STONES
OF
DESTINY

To all the Reiths

STONES
OF
DESTINY

⊚

Stories from Ireland and Scotland

Retold by

⊚

with love.

EILEEN DUNLOP

Eileen

POOLBEG

First published in 1994 by
Poolbeg,
A division of Poolbeg Enterprises Ltd,
Knocksedan House,
123 Baldoyle Industrial Estate,
Dublin 13, Ireland

A catalogue record for this book is available from the British Library.

ISBN 1 85371 307 4

Cover illustration by Aileen Caffrey
Cover design by Poolbeg Group Services Ltd
Set by Mac Book Limited in Stone 10/13
Printed by The Guernsey Press Ltd,
Vale, Guernsey, Channel Islands.

For Antony

AUTHOR'S NOTE

Long, long ago, before Christianity was brought to Europe, people sensed mystery in the wild, lonely places where they lived. Like primitive people everywhere, they held sacred certain animals, plants, and trees—and also stones. Nowhere was the magic and mystery of stones felt more strongly than in the Celtic lands of Ireland and Scotland, where natural phenomena like the Giant's Causeway, Fingal's Cave, and huge standing stones must have overwhelmed people who lived close to the earth, feeling vulnerable and small. How easily great stones might be transformed into giants and monsters in the imagination of people who must often have been lonely and afraid!

Some of the stones were moved in pre-Celtic times and formed into stone circles, where religious rites were performed; many others attracted legends of their own. It was thought that spirits inhabited some, and they became known as sanctuary stones. Others, particularly those with holes in them, were believed to have healing power.

Then there were little stones, the kind that could fit comfortingly into one's pocket or be hung around one's neck. No-one who has ever experienced the pleasure of holding a beautiful pebble or crystal in the palm of the hand can fail to understand how these too became endowed with power, to be passed from father to son, from mother to daughter, as charms against sickness, misfortune, and the Evil Eye.

When Christianity came, and the power of the old druidic religion began to wane, no doubt the church would have liked to see the old pagan beliefs wiped out. But the church was also realistic; understanding that many of the old beliefs were too firmly held to be eradicated easily, it Christianised them. The great stone crosses of the early Celtic church bear the symbol of the sun as well as that of Christ, and many surviving spells and incantations combine pagan superstition with Christian belief.

Like all legends, the stone stories of Ireland and Scotland were first passed on by word of mouth. But gradually, as people learnt to write and then to print, they were written down and circulated in book form. Not all the stories in this book come from the earliest period of history, however; it is evidence of the power which stones have always held over the imagination that new stories about them were still being told well into modern times. Even today, belief in their magic has not entirely died away.

Here, then, are some of these stories—of pagan stones and Christian stones, stones of good and evil power, gemstones, gravestones, and stony places associated with giants, mermaids, demons, and spirits. Tales of valour, tales of humour, tales of horror, tales of cunning, tales of grief; nothing is older than stone, and all through history stone stories have been told, connecting the physical world with one that is mysterious and unseen.

A NOTE ON THE AUTHOR

Eileen Dunlop was born and went to school in Alloa, Clackmannanshire, Scotland, near where she now lives. She has published nine novels for children, of which *The House on the Hill* (1987) was commended for the Carnegie Medal, *Finn's Island* (1991) commended for the McVitie's Prize for the Scottish Writer of the Year and *The Maze Stone* (1982) and *Clementina* (1985) won Scottish Arts Council Book Awards. She has also, with her husband, Antony Kamm, written several information books on Scottish themes, and complied two collections of verse.

BIBLIOGRAPHY

The Life of St Columba by Adhamhnán, ed. W Reeves, 1874

Witchcraft in the Highlands, JG Campbell, 1902

Popular Rhymes of Scotland, R Chambers, 1870

Fairy Legends and Traditions of the South of Ireland,
    TC Croker, 1825–1828

Folktales of the Irish Countryside, K Danaher, 1968

The Ochil Fairy Tales, RM Fergusson, 1912

The Fireside Stories of Ireland, P Kennedy, 1870

Scottish Tales of Magic and Mystery, ed. M Lochhead and
    A Kamm, 1990

Highland Fairy Legends, J MacDougall, 1910

The Peat-Fire Flame, A Alpin MacGregor, 1937

Scottish Folklore and Folk-Belief, F Marian MacNeill , 1977

The Festival of Lughnasa, Máire MacNeill, 1962

The Folklore of Ireland, S O'Sullivan, 1974

More Highland Folktales, RM Robertson, 1964

Myths and Legends of the Celtic Race, TW Rolleston, 1911

Folklore of the Ulster People, Sheila St Clair, 1971

St Kilda and Other Hebridean Outliers, F Thomson, 1970

Traces of the Elder Faiths of Ireland, WG Wood Martin, 1902

Irish Fairy Tales, ed. WB Yeats, 1892

CONTENTS

ACKNOWLEDGEMENT

I am grateful to Antony Kamm for translating "The Wine Stone" from the *Topographia Hibernica* of Gerald de Barri (edition of 1867).

The Stone of Destiny

ꙮ

Jacob was afraid. He had cheated his brother, and his brother had threatened to kill him. He knew that his father had sent him away for his own safety, yet here he was, still far from his uncle's house, alone in the wilderness as night drew on. A wolf howled eerily in the distance and, as the sun went down, smearing the sky with angry red, Jacob felt deserted by God and man. Choosing one of the stones that littered the place as a pillow, he wrapped himself in his cloak and lay down, hoping to forget his troubles in sleep.

His bed was hard and uncomfortable, but Jacob was exhausted. At last he slept and dreamt—a bright, clear dream in which he saw a ladder stretching between Earth and Heaven and angels going up and down on it. Then Jacob thought that God himself was standing at his side, and he heard God's voice promising to look after him.

"I am the Lord your God. I shall give this land where you are lying to you, and to your descendants. Your family will grow and grow, spreading north, south, east, and west. I shall be with you, and stay with you until I have done all that I have promised."

"This is a fearsome place," Jacob said to himself, shivering as he glanced round the barren landscape, ghastly in the dawn light. "Yet it is also God's house, and the gate of Heaven."

1

Jacob wanted to do something to mark the place where God had spoken to him. So he took the stone he had used as a pillow and set it up on end like a small pillar. He took a bottle of oil from his pack and poured some over the stone, as an offering to God. Then he set off on his journey once again.

In Westminster Abbey in London, a worn block of red sandstone lies under the seat of a shabby wooden chair. In England it is known as the Coronation Stone, in Scotland as the Stone of Scone, and in Ireland, more mysteriously, as the Lia Fáil or Stone of Destiny. Geologists insist that it is only a slab of ordinary Scottish sandstone, and there are scholars in Ireland who say it isn't the real Lia Fáil at all. Yet it is the subject of legends that reach back through the past of Ireland and Scotland to Biblical times. The story of Jacob and his stone pillow, told in the book of Genesis, was the one that started it all.

Centuries later, monks loved to tell stories, both tales from the Bible and legends connected with it. One of the stories they told was of the stone where Jacob had rested his head as he dreamt of God and his angels. According to that account, the stone was miraculously preserved. Eventually it came into the keeping of a lady called Scota, daughter of the Egyptian pharaoh Cingris and wife of a Celtic king. Her son Goidel removed the stone from Egypt; it was then carried westwards by the Celtic people who finally settled in Ireland. The stone, already ancient and rich in legend, found an honoured place at Tara of the Kings. Here it revealed that it had magical power, the ability to distinguish between a rightful and an upstart king. When a man destined to be king set his foot upon the stone, it roared like a lion with joy.

During the years that followed, Scots from Ireland braved the sea crossing to Albain, where they made their capital at Dunadd. These were the Scottish Dál Riadans, who gave the land where they settled its modern name, Scotland.

In the early part of the sixth century Muireartach mac Earc was High King of Ireland, while his younger brother, Fearghas, had been chosen to reign over Scottish Dál Riada. More than anything in the world, Fearghas mac Earc longed to be crowned on the Lia Fáil. Only then, he reckoned, would he feel he was truly a king. So he sent a message over the sea to his brother Muireartach: "Dear brother, please, please allow me to borrow the Lia Fáil for my coronation. It would mean so much to me. Of course you have my word that I shall take the greatest care of it, and return it to Tara as soon as the ceremony is over."

Muireartach wasn't keen. The Lia Fáil was a priceless treasure of the Irish people, and he had nightmares at the thought of it being lost, stolen, or—worst of all—sunk for ever in the sea. But he was fond of his brother, and wise enough to know that Fearghas's authority depended on his being recognised as a true king. So he stifled his misgivings, and sent a kindly reply: "All right, Fearghas. I trust you. But for the love of God, look after the stone and send it back to me before winter rouses the sea."

The Lia Fáil was wrapped in fine cloth and put on board a curach. The most skilful seamen in Ireland were ordered to deliver the precious stone to Fearghas mac Earc—and bring it safely home.

But alas! Fearghas repaid his brother's trust and kindness with cruel treachery. After his coronation he went back on his promise to return the stone. It stayed at Dunadd, and it is said that King Aodhán of Dál Riada was crowned on it by St Columba in 574.

The Lia Fáil remained in the possession of the Dál Riadans until their tribe united with the Tuatha Cruithne, or Picts. In 848 it was taken by Cionaodh mac Ailpín, King of Albain, to his new capital at Scone. Now the coronation stone of Scottish kings, it lay there until 1296, when it was stolen yet again.

King Edward I of England hated the Scots. They were none too fond of him, either. For years they had been making a nuisance of themselves, riding across the border to burn English farms and steal English cattle, and whenever England went to war the Scots were sure to turn up on the other side. Eventually Edward lost patience.

"I've had enough," he stormed. "I'm going to teach these impudent Scots a lesson, and I'm going to do it now!"

So in the spring of 1296 he crossed the Tweed at the head of his army, and began his lesson by slaughtering the population of Berwick with a savagery that makes Scots blood run cold to this day.

The Scots were brave, and as a nation would survive to fight and win. But 1296 was a black year for them. They were as cheeky as ever, jumping up and down on the battlements of their castles, thumbing their noses and hooting, "Yah, boo, English dogs! Come and have your tails cut off! Bow-wow!" (It was a common belief in Scotland that the English had tails.) But they were completely unprepared for war, and it would have taken more than taunts to halt Edward's progress. Castles fell, towns were put to the torch, and only three months after his invasion the detested English king received a letter that pleased him mightily. It was from John Balliol, the namby-pamby Scottish king.

"Please, let us have peace," Balliol had written, grovelling horribly as he added, "not according to what we deserve, but according to your majesty's loving kindness." A fine message to a man who had spent the past twelve weeks slaughtering Scots! Small wonder John Balliol was nicknamed "Toom Tabard", or "Empty Coat".

Now King Edward was laughing. The Scots were humiliated, and from then on his campaign was simply a triumphal march. Along the way he helped himself to whatever he fancied, and when he returned south in the autumn he took with him the Stone of Scone, the legendary symbol of Scottish sovereignty. The Scots—who had long forgotten that this sacred relic had originally been stolen from the Irish—were furious, and the insult has never really been forgiven.

The stone was taken to London and placed by Edward in Westminster Abbey. There, except for a brief period in 1950-1, when it was removed and hidden by four Scottish students, it has remained to this day, and every succeeding monarch has been crowned upon it. Today no lettering can be traced on its rough surface; whatever the truth of its long history, it is the most ordinary-looking of stones. But it is said that long ago it bore a Latin inscription, which could be translated:

> *Unless the fates be false, and truth be said in vain,*
> *Where'er this stone is found, a Scottish king shall reign.*

If so, the stone remained faithful to its promise. In 1603, on the death of Queen Elizabeth, the Scottish King James VI ascended the English throne.

Callanish

On a desolate moorland ridge on the island of Lewis stands a prehistoric stone circle, approached by four avenues like the arms of a cross. The stones, the tallest an astounding 4.7 metres high, rise bleakly into the windy sky, and it is easy to understand why the Gaelic name for them is Fir Chrieg, meaning the False Men.

Once upon a time, says a local legend, the stones were giants who lived at Callanish. They were truculent, heathen folk who wouldn't build a church for themselves and, when St Ciarán visited them to preach the Gospel, they sneered and refused to be baptised. St Ciarán was peeved, so he turned them all to stone.

Cú Chulainn and the Sea-God's Wife

ᏒᎧ

Cú Chulainn had decided to take a short-cut home through the wood. He had been hunting all day, stalking the red deer tirelessly over the mountains in the frosty autumn air. Now, as the cold purple shadows lengthened and the moon rose, his companions were taking the hounds, and the kill, home by the path. Cú Chulainn wanted to get there ahead of them, to warn the women to stoke the fire, ready for cooking. It had been a good day, and there would be feasting to follow.

As he left the path, Cú Chulainn was feeling hungry, but well and content. He took his health and stamina for granted, and there was nothing in a day's hunting to tire him. So he was puzzled, as he slipped among the trees, by a strange, numbing tiredness creeping through his body. But by the time he realised that some enchantment was on him he was too exhausted even to feel alarmed. At the foot of a pillar-stone in the middle of a clearing his legs stopped supporting him; he slid down, put his head against the rough stone, and fell asleep.

The sleep of Cú Chulainn was deep, but not dreamless. In his dream he knew that he was lying paralysed and defenceless against the stone, and that when two tall, shining women armed with rods strode towards him through the wood, he could do nothing to escape a merciless beating. Even in his dream he felt the pain, and when he woke his whole body was aching as if he had been attacked in reality. Although his friends soon found him, carried him home, and nursed him with care, the great hero remained sick and as weak as a small child. For a whole year he lay in bed, and his family and friends began to despair of his recovery.

Then, one day, a stranger arrived at the house where Cú Chulainn lay ill and asked to see him. Cú Chulainn, who knew he was under a spell, was not surprised, and listened seriously to what the man told him to do.

"Go," said the stranger, who had green eyes and yellow hair, "to the pillar-stone where your sickness began. There you will learn how you can regain your strength."

He disappeared then, and at once the hero dragged himself from his bed and began to walk, slowly and painfully, into the dark wood. When at last he reached the pillar-stone he found waiting a bright-eyed woman in a green cloak, whom he recognised as one of those who had attacked him in his dream.

"I am the servant of Fann, wife of Manannán the sea-god," the woman told him. "It is she who has enchanted you."

"Why?" asked Cú Chulainn—reasonably enough, since Fann was unknown to him.

The answer was smooth, and not reassuring. "Fann has seen you, and fallen in love with you. She also needs your help. Will you promise to help her, in return for the cure of your sickness?"

Cú Chulainn groaned inwardly. The lady who was in love with him was also trying to blackmail him, and he saw trouble ahead, both with Fann's husband, Manannán, and his own wife, Éimhir. At the same time, he realised that he was not in a position of strength.

"What does Fann want me to do?" he asked resignedly.

Fann, the woman explained, had problems. She had quarrelled with her husband, Manannán, and her palace was being besieged by three demon kings, allies of his. "For all her magical skill," said the woman, "Fann cannot overcome these demons without your help. Your reward will be the restoration of your health and the love of the pearl of beauty, Fann."

Bribery now, thought Cú Chulainn. He also thought of Éimhir's probable reaction if she knew of this offer, and groaned again. But his need of healing was desperate, so he said, "Yes." Immediately the pain and weakness left him, the woman vanished, and he was alone by the pillar-stone.

Cú Chulainn had access to the world of the gods. First he sent his faithful friend and charioteer, Lao, to Fann's kingdom to spy out the land. When Lao returned with a good report, Cú Chulainn himself entered a magical bronze boat and sailed over an enchanted lake to the Other World. Before he could enter Fann's presence, however, he had to fight the demon kings who threw themselves upon him in a dense mist, like cold, drenching, suffocating waves. But Cú Chulainn in his strength was invincible, and the demons retreated in the end.

Then Cú Chulainn walked through the gates of Fann's palace, and she came eagerly to greet him, her blue robes billowing and her eyes shining like stars in her beautiful face. Cú Chulainn could not help being flattered by the attention of so lovely and clever a woman, and he forgave her for the pain she had caused him. Needless to say, Fann was delighted with Cú Chulainn. They stayed together for a month, sharing the joys of her enchanted house. Then Cú Chulainn said that he had business on earth and must go home. "But we shall meet in my country," he told Fann before he left her. "I shall be at the Yew Tree Strand, four weeks from today."

"I shall come to you there," promised Fann.

In the meantime Cú Chulainn's wife, Éimhir, had discovered what was going on. Over the years she had got used to other women falling in love with her daring, handsome husband, and was resigned to his succumbing to their flattery. But there was something in this love affair with Fann that made Éimhir see red, most probably the much-mentioned beauty of the sea-god's wife. So furious was she that she armed fifty of her attendant women with sharp knives. "We're going to kill Fann," she announced. "This is the limit."

Cú Chulainn and Fann had just arrived at the Yew Tree Strand when they saw Éimhir's chariot coming, with the wild and angry women riding behind. At the sight of their knives glinting in the sun Fann almost fainted with terror, and Cú Chulainn knew that he must defend her. Yet his heart was heavy, because he loved Éimhir too, and in hope of avoiding a tragedy he called out to her, begging her to listen before it was too late. Éimhir motioned to her women to hold their hands, and waited coldly in her chariot to hear what her husband had to say.

Cú Chulainn was not tactful. Frankly he explained to his wife how Fann had bewitched him, and how impressed he was by her beauty and skill in the magic arts. "There is nothing a spirit can wish for that she has not

11

got," he concluded sadly.

Nothing of the pain Éimhir felt showed in her stern, stony face. She was too proud to hold her husband against his will, and she loved him too much, she now realised, to kill his new love before his eyes. She ordered her women to sheathe their knives. "The truth is," she said bitterly, "that the lady you have left me for is in no way better than I am. But what is new is sweet and what is familiar is sour, and that's how it is with you, Cú Chulainn." Then, unable any longer to hide her tears, she added words that cut her husband to the heart: "Once we lived in honour together, you and I, and we might do so again, if only I could regain your favour."

Cú Chulainn heard the desperation in her voice, and was ashamed. "By my word, you have got my favour," he told her impulsively, "and you shall always have it, as long as I live."

Now it was Fann's turn to be offended. "You had better give me up, then," she said haughtily to Cú Chulainn.

But Éimhir, half noble and half perverse, shook her head. "Certainly not," she told her husband. "You had better give me up. Since Fann is cleverer and more beautiful than I am, and you love her, it is more fitting that I should be deserted."

And while Cú Chulainn stood helplessly looking from one pouting face to the other, Fann insisted stubbornly, "No, it is I who must go."

Then she burst into tears, so mortified was she at the thought of defeat, and so much in love with Cú Chulainn. But her husband, the sea-god, knew of her grief and, still loving her, felt sorry for her. As Cú Chulainn hesitated, Manannán appeared in a vision to

Fann and said to her privately, "My dear, I am here. Will you come back to me, or stay with Cú Chulainn?"

"Indeed," replied Fann tearfully, "neither of you is better than the other. But I shall go with you, Manannán, because you have no other mate worthy of you, whereas Cú Chulainn has Éimhir."

So Fann went home to Manannán, and Cú Chulainn went home with Éimhir. For a long time he was very sad, but at last the druids gave him a drink of forgetfulness and he no longer remembered Fann. Just to make sure, however, Manannán shook his cloak between Cú Chulainn and Fann, so that they might never meet again for all eternity.

Many years later it was love of another woman, the terrible Mór-Ríon, goddess of battles, that sealed the fate of Cú Chulainn, and again a pillar-stone featured in the story. Knowing that by rejecting her love he had mortally offended the goddess of war, Cú Chulainn went out to a final battle with his enemy, Queen Méabh. Terribly wounded in the conflict and knowing that his end was near, he tied himself with his girdle to a pillar-stone so that he would die on his feet, and with his face towards his foes.

King Frog

At Achagaval in Morvern there was a swamp, and in the swamp there lived a frog. "King Frog" he was called, not only because of his great size but because in his head he had a precious stone. Everyone knew he was there, because they could hear his voice (like a dog's yelping, it was said) from a long way off, even from the summit of Ben nam Bearrach several miles away. King Frog wasn't keen to show himself, however, which was wise of him, because there were many greedy people anxious to kill him for his stone.

The greediest of all was a man called Ruairidh, who wanted King Frog's stone more than anything else on earth. He had spent years trying to trap King Frog, but always the creature gave him the slip. Only occasionally had Ruairidh even glimpsed him, giving a wide, triumphant frog's smile as he slid down into a brackeny pool. All that Ruairidh had learnt in all these years was which part of the swamp King Frog liked best, and this knowledge gave him an idea of a clever way to trap the frog at last.

On a winter day, when there was snow on Ben nam Bearrach and the swamp at Achagaval was covered in ice, Ruairidh left his cottage armed with a heavy stick and accompanied by his tame otter, who was to help him trap King Frog. Making his way over the ice to the place where

14

he was sure King Frog was lurking, Ruairidh cut a hole and lowered the otter into the freezing water below. Then he knelt down with his stick at the ready, and waited for the terrified frog to appear in the opening with the otter's sharp teeth at its back.

But alas! Ruairidh was greedier than he was intelligent, and he had forgotten that otters must come to the surface now and then to breathe. Seeing something move in the hole, he didn't even wait to see what it was. In his eagerness to get hold of the precious stone, he mistook the otter's head for the frog's, and brought down his stick so hard that he killed the poor creature on the spot. Which seems very hard on the otter—though no doubt the frog laughed.

The Rock of the Candle

ᴑᴁ

Once upon a time there lived a hag, the most dreadful hag you could possibly imagine. She had filthy grey hair and a dingy, wrinkled face. Her shaggy eyebrows jutted over eyes that were very small and squinted meanly on each side of a cruel, hooky nose. Her lips were thin, her teeth green, and her chin spotted with horrible tufts of bristling hair. She was also a giant. So hideous was this hag, indeed, that normal witches seemed pretty by comparison, and just as she was uglier, she was more wicked too. Her name was Gránna, and she lived near Limerick on a rock called Carrigogunnel.

The hag had a candle that was enchanted and, as you would expect, not in a pleasant way. Every evening at sunset Gránna hobbled out of the hovel where she lived, set the candle on the rock, and lit it. All through the hours of darkness it burned with a steady, piercing light—which was unfortunate, since the nature of its magic was that anyone who looked at it immediately fell down dead. The hag sat all night long beside the candle, shielding it from the wind and rain. Often she was soaked to the skin, but the fire of evil burning in her heart kept her warm.

Gránna thought that any discomfort was worthwhile if she had a corpse or two to gloat over in the morning, and on most mornings she had. For who, walking in darkness, can resist raising their eyes to a light shining through the gloom? For miles around poor people were bereaved, and Carrigogunnel was a name that made them sweat with fear. "Who can save us from this cruel hag?" they cried piteously, but for a long time the answer seemed to be "No-one." Everybody was terrified of Gránna, and the hag laughed loudly on her rock when she saw the death and dismay her magic candle caused.

At last, however, help came. One day word of Gránna's wickedness and the people's despair reached the ears of the mighty Fionn mac Cumhaill, leader of the Fianna, a company of young warriors who were brave, daring, and ready to avenge the weak and oppressed. They were as little afraid of enchantment as they were of the swords of their enemies, and when Fionn told them about wicked old Gránna their bright eyes gleamed. Immediately they started clamouring to be allowed to extinguish the hag's magic candle, once and for all.

"Let me go," said Caoilte eagerly. "You can trust me, and it would be a pleasure."

"No, it's my turn," pleaded Diarmaid. "I haven't had a challenge for ages. Please, Fionn."

"I'd be glad to teach the old witch a lesson," growled Goll, smiling grimly as he fingered the edge of his sword.

But Fionn said firmly, "No. I've decided that Riagán will go."

"Wonderful!" shouted young Riagán, and the others fell silent while Fionn told him what to do.

"No-one can overcome the hag by courage alone," warned Fionn. "You are mortal, Riagán, and if you were even to glance at that accursed light you too would die." Riagán nodded, his blue eyes unwavering, and Fionn went on: "Magic must be fought with magic. I have a cap here, charmed three times by the magician Lúna of Lochlainn. Wear it when you climb the rock tonight and it will protect you from the candle. From the witch you must protect yourself."

That evening, as the tranquil stars began to shine, Gránna once more lit the candle of death. Grinning, she sat down beside it, unaware that Riagán stood at the foot of the rock, fitting the cap of enchantment over his golden hair. As the young man began to climb silently, so strong was the lure of the weird candle that, try as he might, he could not resist lifting his eyes towards it. But instantly the charmed cap fell forward over his eyes, cutting out the light.

The rock was steep and smooth, but Riagán was fearless and climbed with eager, cat-like skill. So oblivious to his coming was the hag that when Riagán suddenly pounced, she was taken completely by surprise. Before she had time to recover he had snatched up the candle and, with averted eyes, thrown it from the rock. Gránna leaped up. A thin scream of loss came from her withered lips as her treasure hurtled brightly through the air, and dropped into the river Shannon like a falling star. A great hissing, like the anger of a thousand snakes, rose from the water as the enchanted light disappeared.

Then the charmed cap flew back from Riagán's eyes. In a flash of alarm he saw the hag, snarling like a wolf as she bore down on him with her bony arms outstretched, eager to crush his bones to dust. In the nick of time he gathered himself, and jumped. A rushing wind took him in its arms and carried him far, far from the rock. Two miles away he landed, and turned to see Gránna in the distance, stamping and shaking her fist in rage and despair.

The hag measured Riagán's leap with her eyes. Then, in a last frenzied attempt to get even, she used her giant's strength to tear off a huge piece of the rock. Poising herself on the edge, she heaved it up and hurled it at Riagán with such violence that her whole body shuddered. From two miles off he could hear her scream in pain. But he knew he had nothing to fear. He was young, and his strength in leaping far exceeded the ancient hag's strength in throwing. The stone soared into the air and fell half way between them.

No-one should sneer at Gránna's failure, however. It was a mighty feat that she performed. After her defeat by the power of goodness and youth, the hag disappeared and was never seen again. But the stone she threw at Riagán remains a mile from Carrigogunnel. Taller than the tallest man, it would need the strength of fifty to move it from the place where it fell. How can we tell that it is Gránna's stone? Because it has the marks of her fingers still clearly printed on its sides.

The Giant's Causeway

෴

The Giant's Causeway, eight miles from Portrush in County Antrim, is truly a wonder of the world. In prehistoric times about forty thousand mostly hexagonal columns were formed by the cooling of volcanic basalt, creating an enormous causeway, or raised path. Some of the columns are thirteen metres high, and the causeway stretches five hundred metres out to sea. Not surprisingly, before humans began to understand the way their world was made, stories were invented to explain something so extraordinary.

Fionn mac Cumhaill was a great hero—so great that some people couldn't help imagining him as a giant. The causeway, they said, was the beginning of a road Fionn wanted to build between Antrim and the Hebridean island of Staffa so that he could walk over to visit his girlfriend, a woman giant who lived on that island.

The Scots who emigrated from the north of Ireland to Dál Riada took their Fionn stories (the "Fenian Cycle") with them. In Scottish legend the name was altered to "Fingal". On Staffa there is another stunning geological wonder, a deep, sea-flooded cave with basalt columns similar to those in the Giant's Causeway. It is known as Fingal's Cave.

The Blacksmith and the Wooden-Crier

൭ൟ

In the Scottish Borders there is a legend that King Arthur and his knights lie asleep in a cave under a hill called the Eildon Tree. When Britain is in her hour of greatest peril they will rise and come to her aid. In the Highlands there is a similar legend concerning Fingal, who is said to lie sleeping with his warriors inside a rock on the Isle of Skye. If anyone is brave enough to enter the rock and blow the wooden-crier, or whistle, which lies beside Fingal, the sleepers will wake and come out, just as they used to be. Only one person is known to have put the story to the test.

Many years ago there was a blacksmith living on the island, near the rock in which the warriors were believed to lie. One day when he was walking by he saw a hole in the rock's surface that looked to him like a keyhole, and, since he had long been curious, he decided that he would try to get inside. After he had spent some time studying the hole, he went back to his forge and made an iron key that he thought would fit.

The following morning, when no-one was around, the blacksmith returned to the rock. Nervous but excited, he put his key in the hole, and, sure enough, when he turned it he heard the grinding sound of a lock opening. A great stone door swung back silently, and the blacksmith peered into a dark cave. His eyes widened in wonder as he made out a number of huge men, sprawling on the floor. The sound of their heavy breathing was like waves breaking on the shore.

A little apart, lay a man even more enormous than the others, and the blacksmith saw, on the ground by his side, a hollow wooden tube about the size of a small tree trunk.

"That must be the wooden-crier," said the blacksmith to himself, "though I'm not sure that I can lift it, let alone blow it." He lingered a while by the door, looking at the strange scene and trying to pluck up courage; but at last, thinking that if he had come this far it would be a pity now to abandon the challenge, he stepped forward. Picking his way carefully among the gigantic limbs, he stood at the end of the wooden-crier. There was a stuffy, fleshy smell that disgusted him, but he bravely heaved up the instrument, put his lips to the end, and blew with all his might.

The noise was appalling, a strident braying so loud that the blacksmith feared the rock would split, and the hillside above fall in on top of him. The giants on the floor shook from the tops of their heads to the soles of their feet. Too confused by shock to consider what he was doing, the blacksmith gave a second blast on the wooden-crier, then watched in horror as the huge creatures turned over, stretched, and sat up on their elbows. These were not golden youths from the age of heroes; their fingers were like the prongs of wooden forks, their arms and legs like beams of blackened bog-oak. They exuded an ancient smell, and as they opened cold grey eyes as big as apples, the blacksmith's chest almost burst with terror. Dropping the wooden-crier on the floor, he used the last of his strength to leap towards the door.

As he reached it, breathing in a blessed lungful of cold, fresh air, the blacksmith heard behind him an ominous clash of armour. Then there was groaning and the crying of piteous voices in his ears:

"A curse on you, blacksmith! Why did you wake us, if you meant to leave us again?"

But the blacksmith paid no heed. Pushing with all his might he slammed the great stone door and leaned against it. Sweat was pouring from his body like a mountain stream. With a final burst of energy he took the key he had made out of the hole and, running swiftly, threw it into a deep loch nearby. The place is called the Loch of the Smith's Rock to this day.

Glenlyon

Glenlyon, in Perthshire, is scattered with circular castles made entirely of dry stones. Long ago people believed that these were built by Fingal, or Fionn. An old verse tells that

> *Fionn had twelve castles*
> *In the crooked glen of stones.*

The Green Glaistig

෨෧

Of all the weird creatures that inhabited the Highlands of Scotland in bygone days, none was stranger than the glaistig, a thin wraith of a woman with yellow hair reaching her heels and a green dress. From the colour of her clothing and the greyish-green of her skin she was known as the Green Glaistig. A solitary creature, she usually attached herself to a dairy farm, and helped with the herding of cattle.

There was a resident glaistig on a farm in Glen Duror of Appin, in Argyll. Tenants came and went, but the glaistig stayed put. Despite her terrible face, described by those who had seen her as resembling "a grey stone overgrown with lichen", this glaistig proved an asset on the farm. She helped with the herding and the milking, asking no reward except a nightly supply of milk, which was poured by the farmer's wife into the hollowed top of Clach na Glaistig, the glaistig's stone.

Unfortunately there came to the farm one day a new family who didn't believe in glaistigs, and reckoned that it was a waste of good milk to pour it into the hollowed stone by the gate. The glaistig was swift to take revenge. Next morning the calves, which had been carefully penned apart from their mothers to preserve the milk supply, were found in the same field as the cows.

They had sucked their mothers' udders dry, and there was not a drop of milk left for the family's porridge!

On this same farm there was a servant girl who, when asked if she was afraid of offending the glaistig, burst out laughing at so absurd an idea. She too was immediately punished. In the twilight, as she walked to the stream to fetch a bucket of water, she received a slap on the cheek so hard that it twisted her neck. All the next day she looked to the left, because looking in front was impossible. The next evening, however, as she again went to the stream, she received an even harder slap on her other cheek, which set her head right again.

From "St Patrick's Hymn"

I bind myself today to the virtue of Heaven,
In light of Sun,
In brightness of Snow,
In splendour of Fire,
In speed of Lightning,
In swiftness of Wind,
In depth of Sea,
In stability of Earth,
In compactness of Rock.

Columba and the Stone of Power

✹

After the great Irish saint Columba had tramped more than a hundred dangerous miles up the Great Glen to visit the Pictish king Brú at Inverness, the worst annoyance he encountered was a druid named Briochán. Columba detested druids. Servants of false gods, they had hindered his preaching of Christianity in Ireland, then they had tried to prevent his settling on his chosen island of Í, off the Scottish coast. Now here they were again, led by the hostile and impudent Briochán, doing their best to hinder his missionary work among the Picts.

Columba was tall and very strong, and the power of God was in him. He knew that he could have beaten Briochán in any contest, but he had to be careful. Although he and the young king Brú had taken a liking to each other, Briochán had been Brú's tutor, and the king thought he was wonderful. It upset Columba to see how the young man admired the druid's paltry tricks, but he couldn't risk offending him. Without Brú's permission Columba could not spread the gospel in Pictland. So the saint held his peace, and waited as patiently as he could for an opportunity to break Briochán's power over the king.

The opportunity came one bright summer morning when sunbeams were poking into all the dirty corners of Brú's great wooden fortress, making the world outside seem cleaner and fresher than ever. Feachtnach, one of Columba's companions from the monastery on Í, came to Columba with an anxious expression in his eyes.

"Father," he said, "I've been talking to one of the Picts who works for Briochán. He tells me that Briochán has an Irish maidservant whom he holds as a slave and treats cruelly. I thought you might want to have a word with the king."

Columba nodded in grim satisfaction. "I might indeed," he said. "Just leave this to me."

Taking with him his friend Comhghall, who spoke the Pictish language better than he did, Columba strode to the king's private room and knocked on the door.

"Enter," called Brú, and Columba went in.

The room was dirty, and there was a nasty stale smell. Columba, who was used to living in the fresh air, was revolted, but carefully hid his disgust. He was Brú's guest, and it was never wise to be rude to a king. Peering through the half-darkness he saw what he expected; Briochán sitting at the king's side.

"Can I do something for you, Columba?" asked Brú politely.

"Not you, sir," replied Columba, also politely. "My business is with your friend Briochán. Is it all right for me to speak to him?"

"To me?" barked Briochán, before the king could reply. His bearded chin waggled and his absurd yellow robes rustled with indignation. "What business can you possibly have with me?"

Columba, who had a very hot temper, would have enjoyed settling the business with his fists. But he managed to say calmly, "This business. I understand that in your house you have an Irish servant, a countrywoman of mine, whom you treat cruelly and as a slave. I demand that you free her immediately."

Briochán's face went scarlet. He wasn't used to being ordered to do anything. But, certain that if it came to a showdown Brú would support him, he replied defiantly.

"Well, I shan't," he spat out rudely. "Why should I take orders from you? I bought the girl, and I'll do what I like with her. So there!"

He sounded like a spoilt child, and Columba now found it impossible to hide his contempt. His lip curled disdainfully, and he gave Briochán a cold, grey look.

"Please yourself," he said quietly. "But be warned. If you refuse my request to set the girl free, you shall die before I leave this place."

Brú and Briochán looked at each other in astonishment, not knowing whether to treat Columba's threat as a joke or not. But they didn't have long to make up their minds. Briochán opened his mouth to make a scornful reply, but not a word could he utter. His eyes popped in terror as he grabbed a glass cup from the table beside him and took a gulp of wine. As Columba and Comhghall left the room they heard a fearful yelp, then the sharp sound of breaking glass.

"Come with me, brothers," said Columba to Comhghall and Feachtnach, who had been waiting anxiously outside. Obediently the two monks followed him out of the dark, musty fortress and down to the bank of the River Ness. Picking his way past the muddy shallows where cattle drank, Columba led the way upstream to a place where the water ran clear beneath a canopy of quivering birch leaves. Jumping down from the bank, Columba put his hand into the water and selected a small white stone. "Take a good look at this stone," he instructed his friends. "God will use it to cure many diseases among the Picts."

Comhghall and Feachtnach stared at the ordinary-looking stone, then glanced at each other. They knew Columba too well to argue, but it was amazing just the same. Before they could reply, however, they heard the thud of approaching hooves. Two horses came galloping up, their riders sweating and red-faced with excitement.

"I've been expecting this," remarked Columba calmly.

"Columba!" cried the foremost rider, reining in his horse. "I have a message from the king! Briochán is very ill. His face is purple and he can scarcely breathe. The king thinks he will choke to death."

"And we're to tell you," shouted the second man, "that Briochán is willing to release his Irish servant. Will you come now, in the king's name, and cure his friend?"

Columba smiled, and dropped the white pebble into Feachtnach's hand. "Take this stone to the king," he said. "Tell him to put it in a cup of water and give Briochán the water to drink. If he really means to keep his promise, he will be healed."

Then, as if the matter no longer concerned him, he rambled off upstream among the trees. Comhghall and Feachtnach hurried away in the opposite direction.

When the two monks arrived, somewhat out of breath, they found the fortress swarming with Picts. Word of Briochán's predicament had spread rapidly. The chief druid was feared and disliked, and not everyone who had hurried to the king's apartments had come to sympathise. The monks had to force their way among the excited, whispering folk thronging the outer rooms and passages to reach Brú's little chamber. They found Briochán lying on a couch with a cushion under his head, and Brú hovering helplessly at his side. The druid was a sorry sight. His face was an unlovely blue and his eyes bulged like dark plums. Saliva dribbled horribly into his beard.

"Where is Columba?" sobbed Brú when he saw Comhghall and Feachtnach in the doorway. "I wanted Columba to come."

Comhghall felt sorry for the young man, and addressed him fluently in his own language: "Don't worry. We have Columba's authority to cure your friend, provided we have his promise to free the Irish maid."

From his couch Briochán made gurgling noises, but managed to nod his terrible head.

"He will," said Brú eagerly. "You have his word, and mine."

"Good," said Comhghall, and he gave the king Columba's instructions while Feachtnach dropped the pebble into his outstretched hand.

The monks were aware of brown-eyed, curious onlookers in the doorway, but they didn't try to disperse them. The more witnesses there were to Columba's triumph over Briochán, the better. With trembling hands Brú lifted the cup of water with which he had been trying to revive the druid, and dropped the stone into it.

"It floats," he said incredulously, as the white pebble bobbed like a nut in the water.

"Columba has blessed it," said Feachtnach solemnly.

It was the only explanation he could think of. Brú nodded gravely, then bending over Briochán he carefully poured a little water between the thick blue lips.

The result was rapid and astounding. As the king, the monks and the crowd in the doorway watched, the horrible choking noises ceased, and the druid's blue face changed in seconds from purple to mauve, and from mauve to its usual dingy pink. As Briochán began to breathe normally, his eyes seemed to shrink in their sockets. Then he sat up, swung his legs over the edge of the couch, and got to his feet.

A sigh, partly of amazement and partly, truth to tell, of disappointment, rose from the onlookers at the door. The news ran in whispers through the crowd, which melted away as quickly as it had formed.

In the king's little room the druid faced the monks. He was furious, but he had had a bad fright and his self-confidence was shaken. Confronted by Columba's superior power, a sullen pout was all the defiance he could muster. Words failed him.

"Now," said Comhghall, who had an authority of his own, "I am going to come home with you, so that you can free the Irish girl in my presence. And please don't even consider trying to trick me, because if you do you'll find yourself choking again. Understood?"

"Understood," muttered Briochán churlishly.

Charm of a Healing Stone

Let me dip thee in water,
Thou yellow, beautiful gem of power!
In water of the purest wave
Which was kept pure by Bridget.

In the name of the Apostles twelve,
In the name of Mary, Virgin of virtues,
And in the name of the High Trinity
And all the shining angels.

A blessing on the gem,
A blessing on the water,
A healing of all bodily ills
To each suffering creature.

Stones of Iona

❀❀

Legend says that the floating stone that cured the druid Briochán also cured other Picts of all sorts of diseases. King Brú was very impressed and gave orders that the stone should be preserved carefully, because one day he was sure to need it himself. This selfish precaution did him no good, however, as on the day of his death the stone mysteriously disappeared.

Columba's island of Í, later known as Iona, was famous for its stones both great and small. Many kings and princes wanted to be buried there, believing that their sins would be wiped out if they were buried in such a holy place. On the island an ancient burial ground, Reilig Odhràin, can still be seen, at the end of a pathway called the Street of the Dead. Mainly because of Columba's reputation, but perhaps partly because of the royal connection, long ago an oath sworn on an Iona stone was as sacred as one sworn on the Bible.

Columba's monastery was built of wood, so all traces of it have long since disappeared. The only remaining relic of the saint is a fragment of stone that he is said to have used as a pillow.

On the island there are several carved stone crosses, some more than a thousand years old. Before the Reformation in the sixteenth century there were probably more than sixty of these but the new Protestants, who hated crosses, had them uprooted and thrown into the sea.

Most charming of all the stones of Iona are its pebbles. On the beaches, particularly in the bay known as Port na Curaich (Harbour of the Curach), where Columba is supposed to have landed from Ireland in 563, beautiful pebbles can be found—red, white, violet, grey, and green. Long believed to have healing power, these stones in the Middle Ages were blessed and placed on the altar in the Abbey Church. The green ones were also thought to save people from drowning. They were worn as lucky charms, and those who possessed them believed themselves under the protection of Columba.

Halloween Story

✺

So long ago that Scotland was still an independent kingdom at the time, there lived in the village of Tullibody a farmer whose name was Davie Rae. When he was young, Davie had fallen in love with a beautiful young woman named Janet Coklay and, although he knew she was vain and overfond of fine clothes and jewellery, had decided to marry her. For a time they were happy together, but as the years passed and her beauty faded Janet's need for admiration and attention seemed to grow. She smirked and swaggered and flirted with every man she met, and Davie, living at a time when the Scots were very sober and God-fearing, was deeply shocked by her behaviour. Nothing he said made any difference. Janet tossed her head and did as she pleased.

Then one day, when Davie was out ploughing the fields that stretched between Tullibody and the Ochil hills, a very strange thing happened. As he turned the plough at the end of a furrow he saw a quaint little man sitting on a stone. From his green suit and red hat Davie recognised him as one of the fairy folk, and bade him a respectful "Good day."

"And good day to you too, Davie," replied the little man in a friendly tone. "Tell me, how is your wife getting along?"

Davie sighed and shook his head. "Not well at all,"

37

he confessed.

"Is she as headstrong and foolish as ever?"

Davie wondered how, since they had never met before, the fairy was so well informed. But he knew that such beings had strange powers, so he answered truthfully: "Aye, man, she is. If I ask her to do something she'll be sure to do the opposite. I just wish someone would tell me what to try next."

The little fellow nodded his head slowly. "My name is Red Cap," he said, "and I can advise you, Davie. Take this elf-stone and put it in your wife's broth. It will help to make her sensible, you may be sure." And pressing a small, smooth green stone into Davie's hand, Red Cap disappeared.

Davie looked down at the stone and scratched his head in bewilderment, wondering if he had been dreaming. But the stone seemed real enough, so when he got home and his wife was out in the yard, he surreptitiously dropped it into a pot of broth that was simmering over the fire. But as luck would have it, when Janet was pouring the broth from the pot into a dish the little stone made a sharp, clinking noise. Quick as a wink she fished it out, and stood scowling as she examined it in the palm of her hand.

"What's this?" demanded Janet angrily. "Who's been putting an elf-stone in my pot? If I could lay hands on him," she added with a suspicious glare at her husband, "I'd soon give him a hot ear for his trouble!"

Naturally Davie didn't own up. Janet opened the kitchen door and threw the stone into a stream that ran nearby, then they sat down in silence to their evening meal.

Later that night one of their neighbours, Sandy

Short, called in, drunk and making a dreadful din. While Janet sat laughing and encouraging him, he broke into the pantry and helped himself to food and ale. Then he trod on the cat, upset the jug of milk, and sat down on a tray of eggs. In the end Davie had to take him by the collar, run him out of the house, and bar the door against him.

"You're far too strait-laced, Davie," Janet chided him as she wiped tears of mirth from her eyes.

Davie shook his head sadly as he wiped up the wasted milk and threw away the ruined eggs. It seemed the elf-stone had had no effect on his wife at all. This was proved in the days that followed, as she went on flirting and shocking the neighbours, just as before.

October passed, and Halloween came. As was usual in those days, the night was celebrated with gatherings of friends. Bonfires were lit, games played, and stories told of witches, hobgoblins, and other weird folk. That year Davie was invited to a party at Pendreich, in the hills above Dunblane. Leaving at midnight to walk back to Tullibody, he found the night cold and clear, with a full, sharp white moon. When he reached the part of the road that passes close to the fairy knoll he felt tired, and sat down for a while on a flat grey stone. While he was resting and admiring the stars he heard a rustling in the bracken and, turning his head, saw a strange but familiar little figure advancing through the withered fronds.

"Well, now, Master Red Cap," said Davie in surprise. "Where have you come from?"

"From the party at Pendreich, of course," replied the little man.

"I never saw you," said Davie, amazed.

Red Cap shrugged. "That doesn't mean I wasn't

there," he pointed out. "But tell me, Davie—what about your wife? Did you put the stone in her broth as I told you?"

Davie sighed. "Indeed I did," he said. "I put it in the pot, but when my wife poured out the broth it clinked against the bowl and gave the game away. So she's not one bit better. If anything she's worse."

"Ach," said Red Cap in annoyance. "What a pity, Davie! You should have put it in her plate and she'd never have noticed."

"Too late now," said Davie gloomily.

But Red Cap cocked his little head, and with a cold glint in his eye replied, "Not at all, Davie. I'll see you through your troubles, never fear. If your wife hasn't learnt to behave herself by next Halloween, I shall come with my friends and carry her off to our kingdom under the hill." Which said, the strange creature again disappeared.

Davie was not sure how he felt, for Red Cap's words were both a threat and a promise. Certainly there were times, as the weeks went by, when he felt the house would be a pleasant place without his wife because her behaviour got worse and worse. As well as flirting with men she took to drink and made Davie's life a misery with her quarrelling and vile temper. Yet still, deep down, he loved her and didn't want to lose her. He hoped against hope that she would mend her ways so that they could spend their old age together in happiness and peace. But it was not to be.

Autumn returned, and the rusty leaves fell from the trees. As Halloween again approached, Davie began to worry seriously about the fairy Red Cap's words on the road from Pendreich. He remembered the cold gleam in his eye, and he was sure that, under pretence of helping him, Red Cap was plotting mischievously against him. Davie said nothing to his wife, but determined to do all he could to keep her safe that haunted night. With some difficulty he persuaded her to stay indoors, and carefully locked the door and windows before they went to bed. Later he got up and built a huge fire on the hearth, hoping to deter entry by the chimney.

"Now I've done all I can," he said to himself wearily, and went back to bed.

Tired out with work and anxiety, Davie slept soundly. In the morning he was woken by the sun shining into his eyes through the locked window. Speaking his wife's name, he turned over, and looked to see whether she was awake too. He was frightened, though not altogether surprised, to see that her half of the bed was empty.

Doing his best to control his terror, Davie threw on his clothes and went looking for his wife.

"Have you seen Janet? Have you seen my wife?" he asked at every house in the village.

But nobody had. Davie searched high and low that day, and for many days to come, but all in vain. Janet Coklay's neighbours had their own ideas about what had become of her, but Davie had no doubt that Red Cap had done as he had threatened, and carried her off by magic to the fairy kingdom.

In time, the rest of the village concluded that he was right, for Davie Rae's wife was seen, though not by him. One Halloween night some children returning from a party were amazed to see a puffy, luminous cloud sailing over Dumyat, a nearby hill. On it sat Janet Coklay, in the same bonnet and purple cloak she had worn when she lived in Tulllibody.

From "The Fairies"
by William Allingham

High on the hill-top
The old king sits;
He is now so old and grey
He's nigh lost his wits.
With a bridge of white mist
Columbkill he crosses
On his stately journeys
From Slieveleague to Rosses;
Or going up with music
On cold starry nights,
To sup with the Queen
Of the gay Northern Lights...

Up the airy mountain,
Down the rushy glen,
We daren't go a-hunting
For fear of little men;
Wee folk, good folk,
Trooping all together;
Green jacket, red cap
And white owl's feather!

The Fern Fire

In 1791 the minister of Callander, Rev. James Robertson, noted a ghoulish Halloween custom practised in the villages of Perthshire at that time. At sunset on the last night of October a fire was lit, made entirely of ferns gathered during the day. The villagers assembled and, starting with the eldest present, each placed a marked stone at the edge of the ashes. When a circle had been made around the site of the fire it was abandoned, everyone going silently home. Next morning they all returned. If anyone found his footprint in the ashes and his stone removed out of its place, he knew he was doomed to die before twelve months had passed.

The Giant's Stairs

୭⊘

Long ago, in the days of King Philip of Spain, there lived a couple in Ireland called Maurice and Margaret Ronayne. They had a fine mansion between Passage West and Cork and they were very rich, but the only treasure they prized was the son they had named after the Spanish king. Philip Ronayne was a dear little soul, happy, handsome, and clever. For seven years he made his parents' lives bright with happiness and pride. Then one summer day, something dreadful happened. Philip disappeared.

At first his parents didn't worry too much. They were sure the child was hiding, and not until they had looked for him all over the house and garden, calling "Philip! Come out, wherever you are!" did they really begin to panic. Search parties were sent out to comb the land for miles around, while the poor parents sat holding hands on a sofa, too frightened even to cry. Despite the offer of a large reward, however, no news of the missing boy was ever received. Grief-stricken, Mr and Mrs Ronayne retreated behind locked doors, and the servants were afraid to mention Philip's name.

At the same time there lived, not far away at Carrigaline, a blacksmith whose name was Robert Kelly—Robin to his friends. He was a good tradesman, shoeing horses well and making the best plough-irons in the district. He was also a brave and popular man.

Strangely—for he scarcely knew the Ronaynes—on the eve of the seventh anniversary of Philip's disappearance, Robin Kelly had a dream. In it Philip Ronayne appeared to him, a tiny figure mounted on a white horse. To Robin's amazement, Philip told him that he had been spirited away from home by the giant Mahon mac Mahon, and forced to serve as a page at his court beyond the Giant's Stairs.

"For seven years I have never seen the light of day, Robin," said the boy, "but now my time of service to the giant is over. If you release me tomorrow night I promise you will be very well rewarded."

"And how am I to know," asked Robin doubtfully, "that this is not simply what it seems, a dream?"

The boy laughed. "Why, take this for a token," he said mischievously, at which the horse lifted its right hind leg and gave Robin such a kick on the forehead that he roared with pain. Horse and boy vanished, and the blacksmith woke cursing in the dark. When he had lit a candle, however, and examined his reflection in the burnished lid of a cooking pot, he was not very surprised to see that above his right eye, as red as blood, was the perfect print of a horseshoe. Robin blew out the candle and went back to bed, very thoughtfully indeed.

Like everyone else in the district, Robin was well acquainted with the Giant's Stairs. They would have been hard to miss. Massive slabs of stone that rose like monstrous steps from deep water beside the cliff of Carrigmahon, they were said to date from the time of Fionn mac Cumhaill. Robin also knew the local tradition that credited their building to the giant Mahon mac Mahon, who was still believed by some to live deep in the cliff, behind a magic door that would open at midnight for anyone courageous enough to seek it. The blacksmith had never paid much attention to such tales, but now, touched by the child's plight and with the evidence of his injury to convince him, he decided to put his dream to the test. Having made up his mind, he went back to sleep.

Next day it occurred to Robin that it might be sensible, in view of the risk he was taking, to go armed to Carrigmahon. He owned no weapon, his fists having served him for all the fighting he'd ever had to do, so he chose a plough-iron from his forge. When, in the cool of the evening, he trudged off through the glen to Monkstown, he took it with him, slung over his shoulder. At Monkstown he met a friend who offered to row him across to the Giant's Stairs. Just before midnight Robin found himself standing on a little shelf of rock, with the black water slapping softly at his feet. It was very cold.

"I must be crazy," he said crossly to himself, "coming to such a place on the strength of a dream." But before he could call after his friend to return, midnight came, and a faint glimmer of light appeared on the surface of the cliff. Gradually what first appeared as a thin, vertical white line widened, until a porch large and grand enough for a royal palace opened up, level with the water.

"Here I go, then," said Robin. Clutching his plough-iron, he took a deep breath, and hopped from the ledge into the doorway.

What a strange place it was! The walls of the porch at first seemed solidly carved with grotesque, forbidding faces, but as Robin stared they became fluid, and melted into one another. A chin became a forehead, a glaring eye a gaping mouth, a beard a mane of waving hair. The longer Robin looked, the more horrific this sharing and interchanging of features became, and the savagery of the stony countenances threatened to reduce him to mindless panic. But as the door closed behind him the faces faded. Robin felt himself invisibly pushed and found himself stumbling down a dark, slippery passage. A deep, rumbling noise was followed by a hollow "Boom" as the door finally closed. The sound dismayed Robin greatly, but before he had time to rage at his folly in bringing himself to such a pass, he saw a twinkling light ahead, pure and clear as a single star. To go back was impossible, so he went on. The light grew and strengthened, and at last he emerged into a great hall. It was hewn from the rock and lit by a solitary hanging lamp—the star that had guided him to this dreary destination.

In the middle of the room was a massive stone table, around which sat seven giants, as grey and motionless as if they had themselves been hewn from stone. At the head of the table sat the chief giant, Mahon mac Mahon, who had been there so long that his grey beard had actually taken root and, through many centuries, grown into the stone slab. What happened next would have made Robin laugh had he not been almost fainting with terror. Mahon, facing the door, was the first to see the intruder.

"What do you want?" he bellowed, leaping to his feet and forgetting, in his surprise, that his beard was now part of the table. Then, as beard and table separated suddenly, there was an ear-splitting crash. The table fell back on its supports and shattered into a thousand pieces.

Robin's heart was beating like a drum, but he kept his head and answered the giant's question. Tightening his grip on his plough-iron, he spoke out as boldly as he was able.

"I have come," he said, "to claim Philip Ronayne, whose time of service to you ends tonight."

He half expected the giant to pick him up and squeeze him to pulp, but Mahon merely scowled and fingered his tatters of beard. "Is that so?" he said. "Who sent you here?"

"No-one," replied Robin. "I came of my own free will."

The giant nodded slowly. "Very well," he said. "But you must single him out from among my pages, and if you choose the wrong boy you must pay for the mistake with your life. Come with me."

Here was another worry for poor Robin, but he had come too far to change his mind. He followed Mahon from the hall into another one, even larger and much more brightly lit. Along each side were row upon row of pale, beautiful children, all apparently seven years old and all dressed alike, in green.

"Look at them," commanded the giant. "Take Philip Ronayne if you can—but remember, you have only one choice."

Now Robin was close to despair. There were hundreds of children here, and he had only seen Philip Ronayne once, in a dream. Still, he managed to walk along the rows as if it were only a matter of time before he found a well-known face, and tried not to notice the fearful clashing and clanking of the giant's iron clothes—or the size of the hands waiting to seize him if he pointed to the wrong boy. They had almost reached the end of the last row when it occurred to Robin that he had only one option left. He must see whether Mahon was susceptible to a bit of dishonest flattery.

"What fine, healthy-looking children these are, to be sure!" he remarked, casting an admiring eye at the poor, thin little faces. "It's a wonder, considering how long it is since they saw sunlight and smelt fresh air. How tenderly your honour must look after them!"

It worked! Something resembling a smile appeared on the giant's cruel face, and the great head nodded graciously.

"Very true," agreed Mahon, "and I'm sure not one of them would dare to deny it. But it's kind of you to mention it, for it's little thanks I get from anyone for my trouble. So give me your hand! I do believe you're an honest man!"

He held out a vast grey paw, but the last thing Robin intended was to risk his fingers in such a bone-crushing grasp. So instead he held out his plough-iron, and the giant, whose eyesight was poor, seized it. Round and round he twisted it until it resembled a spring. Then he threw it from him, and looked amazed that Robin didn't fly after it into a corner of the room.

The children, who in spite of everything hadn't lost their sense of humour, were greatly amused by the sight of their master shaking hands with a plough-iron. Shouts of laughter rang through the subterranean hall. In the midst of the hilarity Robin thought he heard his name called; he wasn't absolutely certain but, because now he must choose for good or ill, he put his hand on the shoulder of the boy he thought had spoken. "Let me live or let me die," he cried, "but this is young Philip Ronayne!"

The laughter ceased. "Oh, yes, it is Philip! Lucky Philip Ronayne!" sighed the children, and in an instant the hall was dark. There was a rumble as of falling rock, and an icy wind caught up Robin, blasting him fiercely through the dusty air. But he held tightly to Philip Ronayne, and as the dawn broke he found himself sprawling at the top of the Giant's Stairs with the boy in his arms.

"Please take me home now," Philip said.

So Robin did.

The Flagstone of the Fire

֍

On the island of Innishmurray, off the Sligo coast, stands a ruined church dedicated to St Molaise. According to legend, the church once contained a miraculous flagstone, Leac na Tine, the flagstone of the fire. Hundreds of years ago, monks kept a fire burning night and day on this stone as a service to the islanders. In later times, when the monks were gone, a householder who needed kindling for his fire could place a stick on the holy hearth and be sure that it would burst immediately into flame.

One day an ignorant and mannerless Scotsman visited the church, and to the horror of the islanders he used the sacred stone as a lavatory. Outraged, the islanders prayed to St Molaise, who, though usually considered a gentle, placid character, was as shocked as they were. He spoke to God, who acted immediately. A blast of supernatural fire burst from the flagstone, and, before he had time to realise his peril and run, the ungodly Scotsman was reduced to cinders.

Father Cuddy

This is the story of Father Cuddy, who lived in a monastery on the island of Innisfallen in Killarney at the end of the fifteenth century. At least, that was the situation at the beginning of the story.

Father Cuddy and his fellow-monks were as fine a lot of men as you could meet, full of the love of God and gratitude for the good things God provided, including food and drink. None was more grateful for these gifts than Father Cuddy, and none more anxious to please God with a show of appreciation. It would have been a shame, Father Cuddy thought, to give the good Lord the impression that his bounty was despised.

So he ate until his round belly was a neighbourhood joke, and drank until his nose glowed so brightly that you could have used it as a lamp to light you home on a dark night. Because he was happy Father Cuddy looked happy, with cherry cheeks, twinkling eyes, and a smile that stretched from ear to ear. Everyone loved him and he loved everyone, from God in Heaven down to the lowliest creature that walked on earth.

One day a message was brought to the monastery where Father Cuddy lived, concerning a tun of wine. It had been delivered by mistake to the abbey of Irelagh, and the abbot there wanted to arrange for its journey to Innisfallen.

"One of our company must go at once to Irelagh," said the prior when he read the message, "and arrange for the wine to be brought to us here. Whom can I trust with such an important task? You, I think, Father Cuddy. With your love of good wine, I'm sure you're the best man to deal with the matter."

Father Cuddy nodded eagerly. "Certainly, Father Prior," he said. "I shall set out first thing tomorrow morning. Such vital business requires the utmost speed."

So, as the next day's dawn crimsoned the lake, Father Cuddy rowed the monastery's little boat across the gently rippling water towards the peninsula where the abbey of Irelagh stood. Climbing carefully ashore, he tied up the boat in the shelter of a rock and began to walk slowly, and with his usual stout dignity, towards the abbey.

It was a perfect summer morning, still pleasantly cool, but with the promise of glorious warmth to come. Bees hummed busily in the sweet-smelling thyme, and a lark climbed tunefully into the blue sky. As Father Cuddy walked along he gave thanks to God for the beauty of the day, and for the dinner he knew he would be offered by the hospitable brothers of Irelagh. Timing his arrival well, he was delighted as he approached the courtyard to catch the delicious scent of roasting venison floating from the kitchen window.

"Welcome, Father Cuddy," said the abbot, hurrying out to meet him. "Grace be with you!"

"Let it be grace before meat, then!" laughed Father Cuddy. "A long walk always makes me hungry, and I'll swear I've walked nearly half a mile this morning—not to mention crossing the water."

It took only a few moments to see off two of the

abbey servants, carefully carrying the tun of wine. This business concluded, Father Cuddy allowed himself to be conducted to the refectory. There, a smoking platter of succulent venison was placed on the table before him, along with mutton pasties, fresh bread, and a large jug of the monks' best ale to wash the meal down. And when, before his departure, Father Cuddy was offered a glass of whiskey "for the road," he saw no reason to refuse, or to refuse the second, the third, or the fourth.

Indeed, he stayed so long that it was almost nightfall before he set out for home, praising God for his goodness and quickly losing his way among the bushes. Away he rambled in the wrong direction, crashing through the trees and wondering vaguely why it was taking him so long to reach the lakeside. Far be it from me to suggest that Father Cuddy was drunk. There must have been another reason why, as night drew on, he could see two moons in the sky.

"Bless my soul!" said Father Cuddy in amazement. "Nothing in the world is as it used to be!" Then something very peculiar happened.

In a village not far from Innisfallen there lived a young woman called Margery who fried a very good egg, and often, when good works called Father Cuddy in that direction, he would stop at her house to sample half a dozen. Imagine his astonishment when now, some distance in front of him, he seemed to see this same Margery, very pretty in a floating white dress. Since he associated her with eggs, Father Cuddy was surprised to see that she was holding up a bottle, but the sight of it reminded him that he was again thirsty. Forgetting his amazement, he called to her to stand still.

"Hoi! Margery!" he cried. "I can see you, and the bottle.

Stay where you are, my dear, until I catch up with you!"

But the apparition paid no heed. Laughing at Father Cuddy over her shoulder, she moved away from him, skipping through the bracken as the fat priest lumbered after her, begging her to stop and let him have a drink. For miles and miles he seemed to follow until, exhausted and out of breath, he had to give up the chase. Falling on his knees suggested prayer, so he began to pray, and praying, fell asleep.

The day was far advanced when Father Cuddy woke up, scarcely able to believe how stiff and sore he felt. Slowly the moonlight chase after the elusive Margery came back into his mind, and he rubbed his eyes, troubled but still too sleepy to understand why. Then, all of a sudden, he started wide awake.

"Well, bless me!" said the good father out loud. "Is it possible? Last night I saw two moons in the sky, but here are changes stranger by far!"

Fearing that he had gone mad, Father Cuddy stared around him. There were the hills, just as they had been yesterday, and there was the tranquilly beautiful, familiar lake. But everything else was different. Rocks that had stood up sharp and bare were now covered with coats of holly and arbutus. Whole woods were gone, and where there had been oceans of green heather there were now patches of brown ploughland.

Most dreadfully of all, even the season had changed. Yesterday Father Cuddy had walked through flowery grass under a high summer sun, but now the sun rolled sullenly on the horizon, giving neither light nor heat. The ground and Father Cuddy's habit were covered with withered leaves. Icicles hung down from bare branches, and Father Cuddy saw a robin, bird of winter, hopping near him on the hard earth. He was painfully aware that his nose and ears were frozen, and his fingers numbed by the cruel frost.

"Misery me!" sobbed the poor man. "I must get home. I must get home."

But a worse fright was still to come. When, groaning at the cramp in his joints, Father Cuddy creaked to his feet, he saw that he had been kneeling on a flat stone. In the stone were two round hollows, eight inches deep and unmistakably impressions of his knees.

"I know I am not as light as a feather," he thought, "but this is—" *Uncanny* was the word that came to mind, but because he was a monk he hastily changed it to *miraculous*. "I must hurry back to Innisfallen," he said, "and inform Father Prior of this extraordinary experience."

Now Father Cuddy found the right path without difficulty, and within half an hour he was back by the shore. Seeing a boat drawn up on the shingle, he didn't waste time going further to find his own, but pushed it into the water. Frantically he rowed across to the island and waddled breathlessly up to the monastery door.

"It's me, Father Cuddy," he bawled, hammering with his fists on the ancient oak. "Let me in!"

He was so relieved when the door swung open that he scarcely noticed that the doorkeeper was wearing not a monk's habit but a coat and breeches. It was the tone of voice that made him jump.

"Hoi, there, master monk! What's all this noise about, eh? What's your business here?"

"Business?" repeated Father Cuddy in bewilderment. "What d'you mean, business? I've been to Irelagh to see about the tun of wine. Did it arrive safely?"

The stranger frowned and, as Father Cuddy tried to enter, barred his way with a muscular arm. "Away with you, fellow! he snarled. "Don't try to fool me with your monkish tales!"

This was too much. "Fellow!" squawked Father Cuddy, hopping with rage. "Am I to be insulted on the doorstep of my own house? Get out of my way, scoundrel! Do you not see my holy habit?"

The doorkeeper sneered. "Aye, fellow, I see it," he retorted, "and it will get you little respect here. Don't you know that the monks are long gone from Innisfallen? The abbey lands belong to Master Robert Collan, a Protestant gentleman favoured by our sovereign lady, Queen Elizabeth of England. Where have you been if you don't know that?"

Father Cuddy had gone white as a sheet. "Protestant?" he stuttered. "What's a Protestant? And who on earth is Queen Elizabeth of England? Is this a joke?" But he could tell by the man's face that he had never told a joke in his life, or laughed at one. Father Cuddy decided to try another line.

"Look, my man," he said, as civilly as he could manage. "I am the same Father Cuddy who yesterday morning went over to Irelagh to see to the tun of wine. Look at me closely. Do you not know me now?"

In the fading light the man peered at the monk's pleading face, then shook his head. "How should I know you?" he replied. "And yet..."

"And yet?" prompted Father Cuddy eagerly.

The doorkeeper shrugged. "And yet I have heard of a Father Cuddy," he admitted. "My grandmother, whose mother remembered the man, often spoke of a fat Father Cuddy, who had an ungodly liking for fried eggs and was rarely sober. He fell into the lake one night and was drowned, but that must have been a hundred years ago."

At these words Father Cuddy crossed himself and again fell to his knees. "Believe me," he cried earnestly, "I am that Father Cuddy who loves fried eggs, though I'm sure it's a slanderous lie that I'm rarely sober. A hundred years, do you say? Then tell me—what was your great-grandmother's name?"

"Margery Mahoney," the man replied.

"What? Margery was your great-grandmother?" yelled Father Cuddy. "Saints preserve me! I saw her only last night, a wicked creature in white with a tempting bottle. It's witchcraft, after all. But oh! What a strange enchanted sleep I must have had, to last a hundred years!"

The doorkeeper was sure he was facing a madman. Hastily he backed away and slammed the door.

It was said that when he realised his monastery was no more, and that eggs fried by Margery were no longer to be had, Father Cuddy walked sorrowfully to Dingle. There he took passage on a ship bound for Málaga, in Spain. It was not a random choice of destination; Father Cuddy had long been impressed by the rich wine from Málaga. When he disembarked he found a monastery with a good supply, and there quietly passed the remainder of his days. The stone where Father Cuddy slept can still be seen in Killarney, dented by the pressure of two large knees.

The Wine Stone

❧

After visiting Ireland in 1185, a Welsh cleric called Gerald de Barri wrote an inaccurate and credulous but amusing book called *The Topography of Ireland*. The book was written in Latin, and this is a translation of a passage from it:

> *By Cork, in the south of Munster, there is an island on which stands St Michael's, a church very true to the old Christian religion. Just to the right of the main door, and almost touching it, is a stone with a hollow in its top. Every morning, thanks to the saints of the place, there is found in the hollow exactly as much wine as is needed for the celebration of Mass by the number of priests who are due to officiate on that day.*

Hynd Horn

ᗰᗰ

Once upon a time in Scotland there lived a young man called Hynd Horn. He was handsome and brave and good at everything—jousting, fencing, hunting, hawking, harping, and composing songs. Hynd Horn was in love with the king's daughter Jean, who loved him too. They longed to marry, but for all his accomplishments Hynd Horn was only a poor knight.

After he had served seven years at court without attracting the king's favour or any reward, Hynd Horn decided that he must try to win approval in a more forceful way.

"My love, I have to leave you," he told the princess one autumn morning as they stood together on the castle wall. "I must cross the sea and look for adventures, protecting the weak and punishing evil-doers. Perhaps if I become famous for my brave deeds your father will consider me worthy to marry you."

The princess knew how much she would miss Hynd Horn, but she determinedly held back her tears. Even when he told her that his absence would be for seven more years she remained calm, because she knew, as well as he did, that this was their only hope of becoming husband and wife.

"I have a present for you," continued Hynd Horn, and into Princess Jean's hands he put a beautiful silver wand, engraved with three singing birds. "It is your sceptre," he said with a smile, "to rule over Scotland until I return."

The princess smiled too, but as she took a ring with three shining diamonds from her finger she spoke seriously.

"Seven years is a very long time," she said, "so while we are apart you must have this magic ring to tell you how things are with me. If its precious stones keep their brilliance you will know that all is well and my love holds true. But if they grow pale and dull it will be a sign that I am dead, or..." her voice faltered, "married to another man." Hynd Horn found no words to answer. Gravely he put the ring inside his doublet and kissed the princess's hand.

That very day Hynd Horn rode away from the castle, leaving all that he loved behind. Soon he sailed from Scotland to a far country where, for seven years, he toiled slaying dragons, fighting ogres, and helping the sick and poor. Rewarded for his efforts by kings and princes, he grew rich, and news of his valour spread far and wide. During this time, however, he never dared to look at the princess's ring, for fear of finding evidence that her love for him had cooled.

Eventually the years of adventuring were over and, on the eve of his voyage back to Scotland, Hynd Horn at last overcame his reluctance and took out the diamond ring. To his deep distress he saw that the three diamonds had lost their lustre, and looked no better than fragments of common stone.

"Alas," said Hynd Horn to himself, "my dear princess is dead." Then, with a grief that pierced his heart he added, "Or worse, has grown tired of waiting and given herself to someone else." In his anguish he wanted to hurl the ring into the ocean, but managed to hold his hand. "I shall not believe such a thing without proof," he decided. "I shall return to the king's castle as soon as I come to shore."

It was the season of storms, and Hynd Horn was a week on the black, surly sea. When at last the ship reached harbour, the first person he met on the quay was a ragged old beggar who approached him to ask for aid.

"What news of Scotland?" asked Hynd Horn pleasantly as he put some coins into the thin hand. "I've been seven years away," he added, to explain the question.

The old man smiled. "A lot happens in seven years," he said. "I suppose the greatest excitement has been the wedding of our king's daughter Jean just nine days ago. A grand but sad occasion, by all accounts," he went on, not noticing the paling of Hynd Horn's face. "It seems the princess was forced into marriage by her father and will have nothing to do with her bridegroom, for all that he is a king too."

"Why not?" Hynd Horn dared to whisper.

The beggar shrugged. "It's said she had given her heart to one Hynd Horn," he said, "but he went overseas, and is probably dead long ago."

Then Hynd Horn had an idea. "Listen, old man," he said earnestly. "Will you do me a kindness? You will be well rewarded."

"I have been rewarded already," replied the beggar, seeing gold glinting in the palm of his hand. "What can I do for you?"

"Give me your ragged cloak and staff," requested Hynd Horn eagerly. "You can have my scarlet cloak and horse in return." And while the old man was recovering from the shock he added, "One other thing. You must teach me how to beg."

61

The beggar was mystified, but he did all that Hynd Horn asked.

At dusk the following day, wearing beggar's clothes, Hynd Horn hobbled up to the gate of the king's castle and rang the bell. The shutter in the wicket opened, and the porter's round red face looked through. "Well now, old man," he said kindly enough, peering in the half-dark at the bent, hooded figure. "What do you want here?"

Hynd Horn kept his face hidden, and did his best to imitate the beggar's tone of voice. "For Christ's sake, a bit of bread and a cup of wine," he whined. "I am weary with travel and faint with hunger." Then, with his heart knocking painfully on his ribs, he pleaded, "And please, as a favour and for Hynd Horn's sake, ask the bride to come down and hand the cup to me."

It seemed an odd request, but the porter felt sorry for the poor, ragged creature. "Wait here," he said, closing the shutter again.

Hynd Horn stood shivering in the chill twilight as minutes passed like hours. Would the princess come? Would she be altered? What would he read in her dark eyes? Momentarily he panicked and wanted to run away, but Princess Jean's ring was warm in his palm, and he stood firm.

At last he heard faint sounds within. Then the door opened and the princess stood in a rectangle of light. Hynd Horn saw that she was older and graver, but she was as beautiful as ever to his eyes. She was holding a piece of oatcake and a cup of wine, which she silently offered him. In silence Hynd Horn took the cup, drank off the wine, and dropped the ring in the bottom. Then he gave the cup back to the princess.

Startled by the metallic clink, Princess Jean looked

down. Hynd Horn saw her face pale, and her startled eyes trying to see within his hood.

"Oh, tell me," she whispered, stepping through the wicket and putting a hand on his arm, "where you found that ring. Did you take it from a dead man's hand?"

Hynd Horn was thrilled at her touch, but could not help seeing that on her finger there was a gold wedding band. Angrily he shook off her hand and bitterly replied.

"No," he said. "Seven years ago, before I crossed the sea, I got the ring from the hand of a living lady who said she loved me. But now her diamonds have paled, and I know she was never worthy of my love."

The princess gasped at the sound of the voice she knew so well. "Oh, Hynd Horn," she cried, "can it really be you? My father forced me to marry, but I have never stopped loving you." He watched her struggling frantically to pull off her wedding ring. "Now let me prove my love," she cried. "Even though you return to me a beggar, I shall take off my silk dress and follow you..."

Gladly now Hynd Horn stepped forward and took her hand in his. As he did so his hood fell back and she saw his golden hair and beard, and his happy shining eyes.

"Hush," he said gently. "You have no need to take off your silk dress or your jewels. I am not a beggar. I have gold enough for us both, if your bridegroom will let you go."

Princess Jean's bridegroom was a decent man, who had no desire to hold her against her will. In truth, he was secretly regretting his marriage. His bride would not come near him, and nine days of sullenness had seemed like eternity. So the marriage was annulled, and he danced with relief at the wedding of Hynd Horn and Princess Jean.

Maiden Lilliard

∞

One of many battles between the Scots and the English took place at Ancrum Moor in 1545. Having seen her parents and her lover killed by the enemy, "Maiden Lilliard" fought against them in the army of the Earl of Angus. She died and was buried on the battlefield. Later, a stone was erected in her memory with the inscription:

Fair Maiden Lilliard lies under this stane,
Little was her stature, but great was her fame,
Upon the English loons she laid mony thumps,
And when her legs were cutted off, she fought
upon her stumps.

The Doom of Mar

๛

The Earl of Mar was a very important person, the most important in the land apart from the king. He had been a friend of Mary, Queen of Scots. Now, in 1571, he was Keeper of Stirling Castle, guardian of the six-year-old James VI and regent, or ruler, of Scotland. He had a tower and lands nine miles away at Alloa, but he wanted a fine town house at Stirling, close to the castle, where he frequently had to be. Such an important person was used to getting what he wanted, and to getting it straight away.

Unfortunately, in those far-off days the building of a great house was a slow business. The earl was irked by the prospect of having to wait for months, perhaps years, while workmen quarried stone, cut and dressed it, and dragged the blocks on ox-drawn carts for miles along narrow, muddy roads. So when one day he noticed a good supply of yellow sandstone already cut and dressed, only a couple of miles from the site he had chosen for his new house, he decided to take it. That was when his troubles began.

"You remember that land I was given ten years ago at Cambuskenneth, when the monks were driven out?" he asked his wife the same evening as they sat at supper. "The abbey there is deserted now, of course, and already the cloisters are becoming an eyesore. I thought I'd do a good deed, and demolish them before they fall down."

His wife raised her eyebrows. "And?" she enquired.

"And the stone will be perfect for our new house," replied the earl, throwing the remains of a chicken leg to his dog, and smiling in satisfaction at his own cleverness.

The countess, who was a shrewd woman, looked less enthusiastic than the earl had hoped. She pursed her lips as she finished picking scraps of mutton from a bone, and wiped her delicate fingers on her napkin.

"I'm not sure that everyone will see it as a good deed," she warned. "I know the land is yours, but the abbey is a church building, and the monks still have many supporters. Isn't the old abbot still living locally?"

The earl glowered, his face red with annoyance above his white ruff. He hated being contradicted, especially by his wife.

"I'm not afraid of old abbots," he growled, snapping his ringed fingers to summon the page who held his flagon of wine. "The land is mine, and tomorrow I shall give orders for the stone to be moved."

Lady Mar shrugged, sniffed, and helped herself to an apricot.

Some weeks went by. Carts carrying stone rumbled daily over the cobbles of Broad Street and, as the walls of Cambuskenneth Abbey shrank, the walls of the Earl of Mar's new house began to rise from the mud at the foot of the castle hill. People called it "Mar's Work", and the earl felt proud. If occasionally he also felt uneasy, he reminded himself that he was regent of Scotland, and had nothing to fear from anyone. And, for a time, it seemed that he was right. Down on the green bank of the river Forth the cloisters where monks had worked and prayed disappeared, but the earl's new house grew in splendour on the hill.

But then, one stormy autumn night when the sky wept and the wind soughed eerily around the walls of Stirling Castle, a servant came to the earl where he sat alone in his poky room, considering what furnishings he ought to buy. A bed of oak with crimson velvet curtains would look good, he thought, and although the old tapestries from Alloa would do well enough for the hall, he was tempted to treat himself to some new ones. Hunting scenes were fashionable. Perhaps he'd have some of those.

He was summoned reluctantly from his planning by the servant's discreet cough. "Excuse me, my lord."

"Well, what is it?"

"A visitor to see you, my lord."

The earl was astonished. "At this hour? On such a night? Did he give you his name?"

"The Abbot of Cambuskenneth, my lord."

The earl hissed with annoyance. The last thing on earth he wanted was a confrontation with the Abbot of Cambuskenneth, and a fuss about the abbey stone.

"Get rid of him!" he whispered furiously, but it was too late.

Thrusting the servant aside with surprising strength, the old man forced his way into the room. The brown cloak that hung loosely on his thin body glistened with raindrops, and his hood had fallen back, revealing dishevelled wisps of hair. Dark, vindictive eyes looked narrowly at the Earl of Mar.

"Hear me!" commanded the abbot in a hoarse voice. "High as you are, I shall bring you low. Hear my curse, and despair!"

Of course, thought the earl, the old man had gone mad. The loss of his abbey at the Reformation had turned his wits. The sensible thing would have been to summon the guard and have him thrown out of the castle. Yet the earl was strangely curious. "Speak, then," he said, with a scornful smile.

In the flickering light of the tapers on the wall, the old man began to sway to and fro. Then a strange stream of words began to pour from his lips, words that the earl wanted to disbelieve. Yet as he listened, a chill of foreboding ran up his spine and into his hair, making it prickle at the back of his neck. The abbot might be crazy now, but he had been well known as a good, holy man. Could he be speaking the truth? It was impossible to tell.

"Regent of Scotland you are today," intoned the abbot, "but for your sin you will be brought low. Your fine house will never be finished, your title will be taken away, and your lands given to strangers. The place where a king was reared shall be burned. A mother will perish in the flames, the mother of three children who will never see the light. Horses will be stabled in your great hall, and a weaver shall throw his shuttle in the chamber of state." The abbot paused, then added more calmly, "Misfortune, however, will come to an end, though long after you are in your grave. When an ash tree springs from the top of your ancient tower, trouble will be over, and the kiss of peace will be given by a queen."

The earl had risen to his feet, but before he could think of a reply the old man had vanished into the night. Shakily the earl groped for a chair and sat down heavily. Suddenly he felt afraid.

Did the abbot's terrible prophecies come true? Yes, they did. The story of the abbey stone shows the Earl of Mar in a bad light, but he was really a good man. He did not live to see the curse fulfilled. He died a year later, broken-hearted because he could see no end to bloody conflict as powerful men fought for control of the young king. Thus it was his unfortunate descendants who had to bear the consequences of the curse. This is what happened.

When the Earl of Mar died in 1572, the building of his new house was stopped, and never resumed. It stands unfinished to this day.

After the Jacobite rebellion of 1715, the then Earl of Mar, who had fought against King George I and lost, had his lands taken away as a punishment. He became plain Mr Erskine.

In 1800 a terrible fire destroyed the mansion house attached to Alloa Tower, where James VI had lived as a child. Mrs Erskine was burned to death, leaving, among others, three blind children. The family had to move to temporary accommodation, and the tower, no longer inhabited, was put to other uses. A few years after the fire, a company of cavalry was billeted there, and their horses were stabled in the great hall. In 1810 some visitors were amazed to see a lowly weaver working at his loom in the room where both Mary, Queen of Scots, and James VI had sat in state.

After this, things took a turn for the better. Around 1815 an ash sapling began to grow from the battlements of Alloa Tower. In 1875 a descendant of the earl who was cursed was given back his title, and when a Countess of Mar was kissed by Queen Victoria, the Doom of Mar at last came to an end.

A Cure for Headache

∾

An ancient superstition that the Irish and Scots shared with other Europeans was that both humans and animals could be wounded by "elf-shot" (really prehistoric flint arrow-heads). These were believed to be fired in mischief by the "good people", or fairies. To cure an injury caused by elf-shot, a "fairy doctor" was called in, a healer who specialised in ailments caused supernaturally. A bad headache was often ascribed to elf-shot, which was supposed to split the skull invisibly and cause swelling— also invisible—to the head. This is how one Irish fairy doctor dealt with the problem.

First he put a cord round the patient's head and measured it. Then he repeated some magic spells. The third step was to remeasure the patient's head; a shorter measurement (and doubtless it was always shorter) was proof that the spells had worked, the invisible swelling had gone down, and the circumference of the head was back to normal. Next the patient's head was bandaged tightly, and he or she was warned by the fairy doctor to keep the bandage on for several days. This was to prevent the split in the skull from opening up again.

The treatment for cattle was less complicated. A cow suspected of having been elf-shot also received a visit from the fairy doctor. Measurements were made, spells said, and the cow was given a drink of water from a bucket containing a stone axe-head. There was a widespread belief that this procedure could draw sickness out of an animal and transfer it into a sack or a stone placed nearby. It is not recorded how many recovered.

A Scottish Spell for Curing Cattle, 1607

I charge thee for arrow-shot,
For door-shot, for womb-shot,
For eye-shot, for tongue-shot,
For liver-shot, for lung-shot,
For heart-shot all the maist,
In the name of the Father, Son, and Haly Ghaist,
To wend out of flesh and bane
Into sack and stane;

In the name of the Father, Son, and Haly Ghaist.
Amen.

Seoirse de Barra and the Water-Horse

෨

In the parish of Claregalway, between Galway and Tuam, is a heap of stones known as Seoirse de Barra's Cairn. Long ago it was the custom, if someone was passing the scene of a fatal accident, for him to pick up a stone and throw it on a pile. As he did it he said, "The blessing of God on your soul," to the person who had died there. This is the story of Seoirse de Barra, and how he came to be remembered in this way.

Seoirse de Barra and Craoibhín de Búrca were husband and wife, and since each had built a castle, Seoirse at Castlebar in County Mayo and Craoibhín at Annaghdown in County Galway, they were accustomed to divide their time between the two. At Loughnafoor, to the east of Craoibhín's castle, enchanted water-horses lived in the lake. Every night they came out and did great damage to the cornfields with their trampling hooves. Seoirse complained, Craoibhín complained, and their neighbours complained, but there seemed little they could do, since before they were up in the morning the horses had returned to the water. But then one day a blind old man who lived nearby told Seoirse that if he could catch just one of the water-horses he would be rid of the rest for good.

Seoirse asked all the men who lived round about to

come and help, but for a while the horses proved too smart for them. However early in the morning the men approached, the creatures saw them coming and galloped swiftly to the safety of the water. Everyone was getting frustrated and angry, but at last one of Seoirse's neighbours had an idea.

"If we go to the lough after supper," he said, "and hide until the horses come out, we can then form a line along the edge of the water and wait for them to return. Surely we can head one of them off, at least."

All the others agreed, so that night the plan was carried out, and when the horses returned in the morning they found their way to the water barred. By dint of rearing and kicking, all but one of the creatures broke the line, but Seoirse and his friends managed to surround a neat little filly, who surrendered without much of a struggle. A delighted Seoirse rewarded the men, slipped a halter over the filly's head and led her home to the stable. She was as quiet and sweet-tempered as could be, and every day seemed tamer and more friendly to Seoirse and his wife, Craoibhín.

"I have a great longing to take the water-horse out hunting," said Seoirse to the blind old man when he went to thank him for the advice that had saved the cornfields. "She's a strong little creature, and would benefit from some exercise."

But the old man shook his head. "Never think," he warned, "that an enchanted horse would behave in a normal way. You must wait for a year and a day from the time you captured her. Then the spell will be broken and you can safely take her out of the stable."

At first Seoirse took the old man's counsel seriously. He tried to be patient as he counted the days, but when the hunting season approached he began to feel impatient.

"She's such a dear, quiet little horse," he said plaintively to his wife. "Where can be the harm in taking her out and just letting her have a quiet canter through the fields?"

Craoibhín advised him not to, but Seoirse wouldn't listen. Too impatient to wait for a year and a day, he went one crisp September morning to the stable, and put saddle and bridle on the water-horse.

"I shall ride to Knockatoo," he whispered in her ear, "and let everyone see what a fine horse I've got."

Seoirse mounted, and rode out of the castle yard. The sun was rising, and a bronze light burnished the crimson autumn leaves. Thinking that he hadn't a care in the world, Seoirse rode over stubble fields and through oak woods, and whenever he met a wayfarer who said, "Sure, sir, that's a fine horse you're riding," he smiled broadly and answered, "Isn't it, now?"

Up the hill at Knockatoo rode Seoirse, the little filly treading delicately and as good as gold. On the crest they slowed, and Seoirse, thinking that it wouldn't do to tire the little creature on her first outing, turned her head towards home.

The sun was now high in the sky, and the water of Loughnafoor glittered below like a sheet of molten gold. As soon as the water-horse looked to the west she saw the lough, and because the enchantment was still upon her, that was where she wanted to be. With a wild whinny she leaped forward, then away she galloped like the wind, jumping hedges and crashing through bushes in a headlong dash for her watery home.

Seoirse was a good horseman, and for a while he held on, but when they came to a place nowadays called

Leacht Sheoirse (Seoirse's Grave-Mound) the water-horse managed to unseat him. He flew through the air, struck his head on a rock, and was killed instantly. Still wearing saddle and bridle, the horse careered towards the lough, plunged into the shining water, and disappeared.

"The blessing of God on your soul, Seoirse de Barra," said his neighbours sadly as they passed the fatal spot. And each one threw a stone on the cairn in memory of a man who had been brave enough, and foolish enough, to ride a water-horse.

Written on a Cairn near Inverness

The Battle of Culloden
Was fought on this moor
16th April 1746
The graves of the gallant Highlanders
who fought for Scotland and Prince Charlie
are marked by the names of their clans

The Brahan Seer

●●

Kenneth MacKenzie was tired and hungry and annoyed. He was tired because he had spent the whole morning cutting sods of peat and carrying them to the roadside to await the cart that would carry them to Uig. It was autumn now on Lewis, and the cold wind blowing inland from the sea warned that it was time to have the peat stacks built, ready for the winter. Kenneth was hungry because he hadn't had a bite to eat since dawn, and annoyed because the cart that collected the peat was also supposed to bring his dinner.

"It's that woman at Baile na Cille," he muttered angrily to himself, after his third trudge to the edge of the peat bank to look down the empty road. "She's keeping the cart late on purpose to spite me." Kenneth scowled at the thought, pushing out his bottom lip and pulling down his thick black brows.

It might have been true. Kenneth and Mrs MacLeod, the wife of the farmer who employed him, had never been able to live in peace with each other. She nagged and found fault with him constantly, while he returned her criticism with bitter sarcasm. Her red nose, her flat feet, her shortsightedness—nothing escaped the lash of Kenneth's cruel tongue. Recently he had taken to mocking her with her childlessness, which, had he but known it, was going a step too far. Mrs MacLeod was quite capable

78

of delaying the cart carrying Kenneth's dinner. In fact, she had a much more drastic punishment in mind.

Determined that he would not do another stroke of work until he had eaten, Kenneth threw down his spade in a temper. Then, because it was cold and beginning to rain, he wrapped himself in his plaid and lay down to take a nap in the lee of a little hill. He was unaware that the hill was a fairy knoll. Another half hour would pass before the knowledge of such things would be divulged to him.

Kenneth was woken by the voice of Calum, the carter, calling his name. "I am sorry to be so late, lad," said the man apologetically as he tossed down a canvas bag. "I thought Mrs MacLeod would never have your dinner ready, so long she was about the job. I hope she has given you something tasty! But now I must away and see to the peats." Kenneth lifted his black head and watched Calum striding back towards the road.

Kenneth's plaid was silvered with tiny pinhead raindrops, and he was chilled to the bone. Oddly though, there was a spot in the middle of his chest that was colder than the rest of him, and heavy, as if a snowball out of season was lying there. He pushed aside the plaid and felt inside his shirt; as he sat up, something round and hard fell into his hand. It was a stone, smooth and blue as a harebell, with a hole through its centre. Kenneth examined it, then idly closed one eye and put the stone up to the other. Immediately he let out a squawk of terrified surprise.

What he ought to have seen was a circle of black peat and heather, and sea meeting sky. What he actually saw was Mrs MacLeod's kitchen at Baile na Cille, and there she was, in her brown dress and white mutch, preparing his dinner at the table. Her grey eyes were flinty as usual, but there was a most unusual smile on her thin lips as she laid out a mutton pie and two potatoes, and went to the barrel in the corner to draw him a bottle of ale. Then—Kenneth gasped in horror—Mrs MacLeod tiptoed to the window and peered furtively into the yard. He saw her bar the door, scuttle to the press, and take out a small black phial. Quickly returning to the table, she let three drops of greenish liquid fall on the mutton pie, then poured several more into the ale. Corking the bottle firmly, she put it with the food into a canvas bag.

A canvas bag! Almost fainting with shock, Kenneth MacKenzie dropped the blue stone and stared at the same bag lying at his feet. With shaking fingers he snatched it up, undid the string, and threw the contents far away among the heather. With a triumphant scream two seagulls swooped on the pie. They did not rise again.

"The wicked old witch," moaned Kenneth, trembling in every limb. "She nearly poisoned me!" Then he fell silent, staring in wonder at the stone.

Afraid of the storm he would raise if he accused his employer's wife of attempted murder, Kenneth MacKenzie left Uig that very day. Crossing the island on foot, he took a passage from Stornoway to Stoerhead on the mainland. From there he travelled to Loch Ussie on the Brahan estate in Easter Ross. He had been born on land belonging to the Seaforths on Lewis, and it seemed natural to him to move to land where the same family ruled. With the magic stone in his pocket and the homicidal farmer's wife left far behind, Kenneth found work as a farm labourer and began a new life. Superficially it was very like the old one, but it had an extra dimension that made it very different indeed.

With the help of his magical blue stone, Kenneth was able to see into the future. While he continued to earn his living as he always had, working as a farm hand on the land of wealthier men, he became famous throughout the Highlands of Scotland as the "Brahan Seer", a prophet who could foretell events long in advance. Enough of his prophecies came true immediately to establish his reputation, but others came true long after he was dead. As well as strange but trivial happenings such as the birth of a "bald black girl" and a calf with two heads, Kenneth MacKenzie foretold the Battle of Culloden, the cutting of the Caledonian Canal, the coming of the railways, and the finding of North Sea oil, which he called "horrid black rain".

No-one ever claimed that Kenneth MacKenzie was a pleasant man. It seems that he learnt nothing from his alarming experience with the farmer's wife on Lewis, and that he continued in Easter Ross to carp and quarrel and wound his neighbours with his razor-sharp tongue. But no-one can help feeling sorry for him when they hear of the shocking way he died, nor sad that it was his amazing power that proved his undoing. The gift of the fairies became a curse in the end.

At Brahan Castle lived another Kenneth MacKenzie. This one was the Earl of Seaforth, a rich nobleman who owned all the land around, as well as great estates on Lewis and in Kintail. In 1661 the earl set out on a journey to Paris, leaving his wife at home but promising to return in a few weeks' time. Although disappointed at being denied a holiday in France, Lady Seaforth at first made the best of things. It was only as weeks turned into months and her husband didn't come home that she became first uneasy and then angry and suspicious. What was keeping Lord Seaforth in lively, amusing Paris, she wanted to know, while she was stranded, bored and neglected in dismal Brahan Castle?

In those days of poor communications she might have asked this question for ever in vain, but suddenly she had an idea. Even she had heard of the Brahan Seer and his magic stone, and it occurred to her that if anyone could tell her what was delaying her husband, Kenneth MacKenzie was the man. So she sent for him.

At first Kenneth was flattered by the summons. Even the great Lady Seaforth, he thought, was acknowledging his power—and would want to reward him well for his assistance. So, never pausing to remember Lady Seaforth's reputation as a vain, cruel and ungrateful woman, he put his magic stone in his pocket and cheerfully walked the half-mile to Brahan Castle. As he was shown into the tapestry-hung hall, he was feeling very pleased with himself.

Lady Seaforth made her request civilly enough, and Kenneth, with perfect faith in the stone, told her that he could help her.

"If Lord Seaforth is alive," he said rather boastfully, "I shall see him through my stone."

"Then do so," said Lady Seaforth, and watched haughtily as Kenneth took out the stone and held it up to his eye. He then made the worst mistake of his life, which was to burst out laughing. "Well? Tell me what you see!" rapped out the countess.

"Oh, Lord Seaforth is alive and well," Kenneth assured her, allowing a faint, fatal hint of his habitual sarcasm to sound in his voice. "Truly, your ladyship need not be anxious about him."

This was foolish. People like Kenneth were not supposed to mock people like Lady Seaforth, and trouble was bound to follow. Kenneth heard the sharp intake of her breath, and as she moved in her chair the swish of her silk skirts sounded dangerous, like the hissing of snakes.

"Tell me what you have seen!" she commanded with a hard glint in her eyes. "At once, or it will be the worse for you!"

Suddenly Kenneth was no longer laughing. All he had heard of this woman's cold heart and evil temper returned to him, and he was afraid. He shook his head, and turned the blue stone over in his hands. Subdued, he said, "It would be wiser for your ladyship not to question me."

These words, of course, only made the countess more avid than ever to know the truth. Her face went bright red, and she stamped her foot in its little velvet shoe. "Answer me this minute, you impertinent fellow!" she rasped. "Do you not know that in my husband's absence I have the power of life and death over you?"

Kenneth didn't need a magic stone to tell him that. Expectation of reward faded, and he had a cold premonition that no matter what he said, his end was at hand. He decided to tell the truth.

"I have seen the Earl of Seaforth," he said clearly, "in a beautiful gilded chamber." Then he added the words that sealed his fate. "He is making love to a fair lady."

Lady Seaforth drew back her upper lip, revealing sharp teeth. "You vile man!" she snarled. "You warlock! How dare you say such a thing! You will pay for your witchcraft and evil lies with your life!" Then she screamed for two burly menservants, and told them to chain up the seer while his execution was arranged.

The Countess of Seaforth decreed the cruellest of deaths for Kenneth MacKenzie, whose only crime had been to answer her question. In a field near Fortrose a barrel of tar was heated, and orders were given that the Brahan Seer was to be thrown head first into it. Kenneth approached his death with admirable calm, and in the moments before he died uttered his last, most famous prophecy.

"I see far into the future, and read the doom of my oppressor," he said. "I see a chief, the last of his line, both deaf and dumb. He will be the father of four fine sons, all of whom will die before him. He will die broken-hearted, knowing that no future chief of the MacKenzies will rule at Brahan or Kintail." He paused, then went on: "In the days of this last Seaforth there will be four other lairds: Gairloch, Chisholm, Grant, and Raasay. The first will be buck-toothed, the second hare-lipped, the third half-witted, and the fourth a stammerer. When Seaforth sees them he will know that his sons are doomed, and that his lands will pass to a stranger."

Then Kenneth MacKenzie threw his magic stone into a loch nearby, and went bravely to his death.

It seems very unfair that innocent people, more than a century later, had to suffer for the sin of a cruel Countess of Seaforth. But, just like the Doom of Mar, the Doom of the Seaforths came true. In the early years of the nineteenth century, four unfortunate Scottish gentlemen appeared with the handicaps that the Brahan Seer had predicted. Francis, the last Earl of Seaforth, became deaf and dumb after a childhood illness, but grew to be a remarkable man. He raised a regiment of Seaforth Highlanders during the Napoleonic Wars and later became Governor of Barbados. But his four sons died during his lifetime, and he was left alone. As Sir Walter Scott wrote:

Of the line of MacKenzie remains not a male
To bear the proud name of the Chief of Kintail.

Holed Stones

๛

In past times both the Irish and Scots believed that stones with holes through them had the power to heal.

In Brahan Wood, a few miles from Dingwall in Easter Ross, there is a large holed stone called the Garadh Tholl. Children used to be taken there to be cured of various illnesses. A fire was lit and the child undressed; first his clothes, and then the child himself was passed through the hole.

In the river Dee near Dinnet in Aberdeenshire, there is a holed stone known as the Kelpie Stone, credited with the power to change a childless woman into a happy mother. On one occasion a nobleman's wife braved the freezing water to ease herself through the hole, but was disappointed when she did not become pregnant. A wise woman whom she consulted told her that she had gone through in the wrong direction, against the stream. So the lady tried again, going with the flow of the river, and this time had her heart's desire.

At Ardmore in County Waterford is Cloch Naomh Déaglán, St Declan's sacred stone. Instead of a hole through its middle, this stone has a bite out if its base, which makes a tunnel between it and the rock it rests upon. Pilgrims used to squeeze themselves three times through the space, hoping to be cured of pains in the back. It was said that no-one wearing borrowed or stolen clothes could pass unharmed beneath it.

In Aberdeenshire...

The four great landmarks on the sea
Are Mount-mar, Lochnagar, Clochnaben and Bennochie.

The Enchanted Bride

∽

For weeks there had been excitement in the castle, rising to fever pitch as the day of the wedding drew near. Carts drawn by sweating oxen rumbled into the courtyard, and in the kitchen the roasting of meat, baking of loaves and making of puddings went on from morning until night. The bride's father ordered up flagons of wine from the cellar, while high in a turret-room her mother and sisters sat, stitching and embroidering the wedding gown. The great hall was decked with evergreens, and musicians practised their merriest tunes for the dancing that would conclude the happy day.

Only the bride took no part in these joyful preparations. Silent and grave, Maoilín MacAuliffe sat at her bedroom window, gazing out across the valley of the river Dalua to the black rock that rose like a wall from an ancient oak-grove. She could see the church too, where in three days' time she would be married to handsome Eoghan O'Herly, but it was the rock that fascinated her. She couldn't stop looking at the rock. From time to time her mother came to chide her, her small feet tapping impatiently over the stone floor.

"Maoilín, I don't understand you. Every soul in the house is working for you, doing their best to make your wedding wonderful, while you sit here looking as if the end of the world is at hand. What ails you, girl? Have you and young O'Herly not longed to wed since you were barely out of your cradles?"

Maoilín pushed her brown hair back from her pale face and sighed. It was true that she and Eoghan O'Herly had always been friends, true that their childhood companionship had blossomed into what she had believed to be love. How then could she explain to her mother, who was putting the last stitches into her wedding gown, that her feelings had changed since a stranger had begun to haunt her dreams—a stranger as dark as Eoghan was fair, with black, compelling eyes and a smile that said, "Struggle as you may, you will be mine."

At first Maoilín had struggled, but now she was strangely at peace. It no longer even troubled her to know that the stranger, whose face was clearer in her mind than Eoghan's these days, had some uncanny connection with the dark rock that frowned on Castle MacAuliffe from across the ravine. But she could not tell her mother, who would hiss through her teeth with exasperation and tell her not to be a fool. And perhaps she was a fool, for she knew that the stranger had no certain existence outside her dreams.

So Maoilín said, "Yes. I love Eoghan, Mother," and struggled to remember the young man's face.

"Then stop moping, my child, and come down to the hall. Everyone wants to see a happy bride."

On the night before the wedding a fearful storm arose. From the four corners of Ireland the winds came roaring, and hurled themselves against the old grey castle on the hill. Thunder growled and sharp forks of lightning clawed the sky, illuminating the black rock and the violently agitated oak-grove. Then the rain came, drumming like angry fingers on the windows, cascading down the walls.

Just before dawn the wind tore away a section of the roof above the great hall. When the quaking inhabitants of the castle rose on the morning of Maoilín's wedding day, they realised that the marriage feast would have to be held in a place roofed by the sky.

"We must pray that the rain is over and gone," they said. "So inconvenient at such a time."

Only Maoilín, like a beautiful ghost in her white-and-gold wedding gown, gazed up at the patch of turbulent sky and knew that what had happened was no accident. The hole in the roof had a purpose, and before tomorrow she would know what it was.

The rain held off, though the wind continued to roar. Late in the day Eoghan O'Herly and Maoilín MacAuliffe were married in the little church; the young man's face was bright with happiness, his bride's with an enchantment he could not have begun to understand.

As night drew on, light shone out from every window of the castle and music floated from the hall as the guests, splendid in silk and velvet, began to gather for the feast. Maoilín stood with Eoghan and her parents by the door to greet them. She tried to smile and look as if she were pleased with the compliments on her face, her jewels, and her dress. In reality she cared nothing for these things. Her eyes were looking over every shoulder, searching the ranks of the guests for the face she knew she must see. But the stranger did not come to greet her, and she sat through the banquet at her bridegroom's side. From time to time she glanced up at a hole in the roof, but all she saw was a tattered sky and an indifferent moon.

After supper Maoilín danced first with Eoghan,

then with her father, although they seemed like strangers to her now. It was midnight when she saw the familiar figure advancing down the hall, and knew that she had been waiting for this moment all her life. He was smaller than she had imagined, a slim creature in green velvet with gleaming black hair and eyes that smiled a summons Maoilín had no wish to deny.

"Come, dance with me, my lady," he said in a soft, enticing voice, and Maoilín gave him her hand with an answering smile on her lips.

The company drew back as these two took the floor and stepped to the stately music of a pavane. The tapers on the walls seemed to fade and the faces of those Maoilín had loved shimmered and grew indistinct. So deep was her enchantment now, that she had forgotten their names. A great joy swept over her as the stranger gripped her hand more firmly and whispered, "Now!"

Suddenly Maoilín found herself flying. Up into the air she rose, up through the hole in the roof, until she could look down and see the upturned faces of the wedding guests, very small and far away. Then the wind took her and blew her, hand in hand with the stranger, across the valley to the black rock above the oak-grove. As they landed, a door in the cliff face opened. Maoilín saw a soft, clear light, and heard the charmed music of another world.

The Legend of Loch Awe

☯☯

Where Loch Awe now spreads its dark water, long ago there was a green, fertile glen. The glen belonged to Bera the Old, last of a race of giants who once lived in Argyll. Bera loved her glen dearly. She had herds of cattle feeding on its rich pasture, and, aged as she was, still enjoyed hunting over the hills and among the trees.

But Bera had a problem. At the head of her glen there was a spring, which threatened to flood it if left unchecked. Bera had learnt how to control the spring with a heavy boulder. Between dawn and dusk she allowed its water to irrigate her land, but each night at sunset she placed the huge stone over the source, so that the spring was dammed during the hours of darkness.

One summer afternoon, however, Bera was tired after hunting, and fell asleep on the hillside above her glen. All evening and all night she slept, and didn't wake until after sunrise the following day. Horrified, she rose and hurried with giant steps to the spring. Alas, she was too late. While she was sleeping it had gushed from the earth, and instead of her beloved glen, Bera saw spread out below the vast water of Loch Awe.

The Grey Paw

〰️

It all began with a dare. On a dark autumn night when the moon was new and the stars shone coldly above Loch Awe, talk in the taproom of the inn at Kilnure had turned to ghosts.

Everyone had a tale to tell. First the blacksmith, then the farmer, then the drover spoke of a friend of a friend who had passed the graveyard at night and had seen...

Lights flickering among the gravestones, said the farmer. An old woman in her shroud, said the blacksmith. A skeleton with fiery eye-sockets, said the drover. Then they all shivered and drew nearer to the fire, as the landlord remembered how his father had once heard psalm-singing in the ruined church at midnight, and the pedlar reminded them of the human skull grinning in the niche above the door, which they had all seen in daylight with their own eyes. There was a terrible silence, as everyone thought of the dark road home.

Only one man had not taken part in the conversation, and only he looked indifferent now. He was thin and dark-faced, a tailor who lodged nearby at the farm of Fincharn. Putting down his glass, he glanced scornfully round the ring of frightened, firelit faces.

"You're a lot of superstitious fools," he said. "There's no such thing as a ghost."

An indignant babble of voices contradicted him.

"A fool, am I, when it was my own father heard the psalms?"

"Everyone knows the dead rise..."

"Very true. On Halloween..."

"And since you know so much, tailor, will you go now to the ruined church and bring us back proof that you dared to enter?"

Everyone laughed at the blacksmith's words. It was the tailor who was a fool if he dared to accept such a challenge.

"Aye, go on, tailor," mocked the pedlar. "Go to the church and bring us back the skull that sits above the door."

"We dare you," chortled the farmer.

The tailor stood up, drained his glass, and put it down on the bar. "I shall give you stronger proof than that," he said calmly. "Here in my pack I have a pair of trews, cut but not sewn. Between now and cock-crow I shall sew them in the ruined church—aye, and bring you back the skull along with them in the morning. Landlord, I'll trouble you to lend me a candle."

There was silence as the landlord found a new candle and handed it over. Then the tailor lifted his pack, wished the company a cheerful good-night, and left the inn. The pedlar and the blacksmith followed him until they saw him go through the churchyard gate, then they went home to bed.

The tailor was a brave man. If anything made him shiver as he made his way up the overgrown path to the church it was the cold. If anything troubled him it was the prospect of numb fingers as he plied his needle in the roofless building. But he thought he could warm his hands above the candle, and by eleven o'clock he was seated cross-legged on a flat gravestone raised on four pillars, with his candle at his side. Taking the trews from his pack, he threaded his needle by its light and began to sew.

The hour of midnight approached quietly—too quietly almost. The moon went silently up the sky, and there was not a whisper of wind. For the first time, the tailor felt a tiny niggle of doubt at the wisdom of being in such a place at such an hour, but he told himself he was being foolish, since there was no such thing as a ghost. He whistled a merry tune to keep up his spirits, and midnight came.

It was about a quarter past the hour when the tailor heard a noise that startled him. It seemed to be coming from another gravestone that lay between him and the door, where the skull grinned whitely in its niche. Strange, thought the tailor. Glancing in the direction of the sound, he seemed to see the stone move but, reminding himself that ghosts didn't exist, he whistled a little more loudly and went on with his work.

Not long after, however, he heard another sound, this time unmistakable. It was a voice, coming from under the same stone, and in a hollow, quivering tone it said, "See the old mouldy head that is without food, tailor!"

The tailor looked up, and sure enough, a great hairless head with skin like grey moss was glowering at him over the edge of the tomb. Oh dear! he thought. I have not been so clever after all. He felt sweat running down his face, and wanted to drop his work, blow out the candle, and run for his life. But the thought of the jeering faces in the taproom of the inn made him hesitate, and decide to stay. It seemed the dead could rise after all, but this ghost wasn't going to get the better of him. So he said calmly, "I see that, and I sew this," and he stitched a little faster than before.

After a little while the voice spoke again, this time in a louder, angrier tone.

"See the long grizzled neck that is without food, tailor!"

The tailor looked at the neck and shuddered, but again he bravely answered, "I see that and I sew this," then stitched a little faster than before.

A third time the voice spoke, shouting in a hoarse, menacing tone. "See the long grey arm that is without flesh and food, tailor!"

"I see that and I sew this," responded the tailor, though his heart pounded with terror as he looked at the skeletal arm. But the left leg of the trews was sewn and he was half way through the right, so he plied his needle faster and began to lengthen his stitches.

"See the long crooked shank that is without flesh and food, tailor!" howled the corpse, swinging a mouldering leg over the side of the tomb.

"I see that and I sew this."

"See the other long crooked shank that is without flesh and food!"

"I see that and I sew this."

The abomination had its feet on the ground, but there was a streak of light in the eastern sky and the trews were nearly sewn. There was a pause, but then the long, fleshless and foodless grey arm was slowly stretched out towards the tailor. The voice was a hungry whisper now.

"See the great grey paw without blood, or flesh, or muscles, or food, tailor!"

"I see that and I sew this," replied the tailor bravely, but when he glimpsed the terrible, eager paw, he knew it was time to flee. With two long stitches and a knotting of the thread he finished his task, blew out the candle, and sprang to the door, leaping to snatch the skull as he crossed the threshold. In a wave of putrid air the apparition came after him, its hideous hand raised to strike. But the tailor ducked the blow and instead the grey paw smashed against the doorpost, which bears the marks of palm and fingers to this day.

Mercifully, just at that moment the cock crew, loud and earthly in the breaking dawn. It was the signal for the dead to return to the grave, and the tailor went thankfully home to breakfast. Certainly he was sorry to have been proved wrong, but at least he now had a better story than anyone to tell in the taproom of the inn.

On Scottish Gravestones

Here lie the remains of
Thomas Woodhen
The most amiable of
Husbands
And excellent of men
His real name was Woodcock
But it wouldnt Rhyme

Erected to the memory of
John McFarlane
Drown'd in the Water of Leith
By a few affectionate friends

Here lies Andra Macpherson
Who was a peculiar person:
He was six feet two
Without his shoe
And he was slew
At Waterloo

The Vengeful Mermaid

∾

Near Girvan, on the south-west coast of Scotland, the old grey house of Knockdolion reared up above the cold rocks. It was a grim, ugly house, scowling into the wind that blew from the sea, but within there was warmth and happiness, because the lady of Knockdolion had recently given birth to a baby boy. The laird was overjoyed to have an heir to his title and lands, and the mother thought that hers was the most beautiful child ever born.

One thing alone spoiled the young family's contentment. Down on the shore, just below the tideline, was a black stone, and on that stone, night after night from dusk till dawn, there sat a mermaid. The lady could see her from the window, pale and thinly green in the moonlight, her scaly tail glistening against the stone as she combed and combed her gleaming hair.

It wasn't the mermaid's presence that the lady minded, it was her singing. All night long she sang in a high, pure voice. The lady couldn't understand the words, but the notes seemed to penetrate the walls of the house until she thought the clear, unearthly sound would drive her mad. Nor was she alone. No servant would stay long at Knockdolion, because the mermaid's singing made it impossible to sleep, and even worse, the precious baby was awake and fretful all night long. His mother was sure he was losing weight, and she was frantic with anxiety.

"What can we do to get rid of that terrible mermaid?" wailed the lady to her husband. "Why can't she go and disturb somebody else?"

But the laird shook his head cautiously. "We must beware of upsetting such a creature," he warned. "If she took offence, her revenge could be dreadful."

So the lady decided to be polite. That night she put on her velvet cloak and, passing swiftly through the shadowy garden, descended a flight of rocky steps to the shore. There she approached the mermaid where she sat singing and combing on her stone. The mermaid paused, and stared coldly.

"You sing so beautifully," said the lady, hoping she didn't sound as insincere as she felt. "We all love to hear you sing. Only my baby is too young to appreciate music, and I'm afraid your singing disturbs his sleep. If you are a mother yourself, I'm sure you'll understand."

Immediately she realised that this last appeal had been a mistake. At the mention of motherhood the mermaid's glass-green eyes narrowed jealously, and her smooth forehead creased in a frown. But she said nothing, and the lady knew that her plea had been in vain. The mermaid turned her back and, with an insolent flick of her tail resumed her singing and the combing of her long hair. Sadly, the lady went home.

Time went by, and the mermaid sang on until one day the lady, who hadn't had a night's sleep for months, could bear no more. When her husband was away on a visit, she called two of her servants. They came, heavy-eyed from lack of sleep.

"Take hammers," the lady commanded. "Go down to the shore while the tide is out and smash that black stone into a hundred pieces. My child shall sleep tonight, and so shall we all."

The servants were only too eager to obey. With hammers and a pick they hurried down to the shore and smashed the mermaid's stone to smithereens.

"A good job done," said one.

"And high time too," said the other.

That night the lady waited at her window for the mermaid to come with the flowing tide. As the moon rose and shone coldly on the rocks, she saw the familiar head rise sleekly where the black stone had been. The mermaid's green eyes glittered angrily when they saw what had been done, then lifted their gaze to the lighted window where the lady stood. The lady stared back, and for a moment knew triumph, until the mermaid began to sing again. This time, as the words were borne on the rising wind to the walls of Knockdolion, the lady understood them all too well.

"You may think on your cradle—I'll think on my stane, and there'll never be an heir to Knockdolion again."

As a cloud blew over the moon and the mermaid plunged into the surf for the last time, a cold hand seemed to grip the lady's heart.

That night she tried to stay awake, but sleep overcame her at last. In the morning the cradle was found overturned, and the child dead beneath it. The lady of Knockdolion had no more children, and the bereaved laird was the last of his line.

Serpent Stones

In the Highlands of Scotland and in the Hebrides, a stone known as a "serpent stone" is sometimes found among the heather. It was greatly valued in times gone by as an aid for women in childbirth and as a protection against disease and enchantment.

The stone was supposedly formed by snakes entwining themselves, and making a ball of spittle mixed with a secretion from their bodies. When the ball hardened, the hissing snakes tossed it into the air. At this moment a brave person might approach and catch it, since its magic depended on its not touching the ground. It was then necessary to jump on horseback and ride like the wind, since the snakes would pursue angrily until they were cut off by running water.

A Roman called Pliny the Elder claimed to have seen a serpent stone the size of a small apple and "pockmarked like the arms of a jellyfish".

Blue Grass

❀❀

Long ago on a moonless night when Peter, Conall and
Benedict were crossing Ardagh Hill in County Longford,
Conall disappeared suddenly into the bowels of the
earth. The poor man didn't even have time to cry out, and
his companions had gone a little way before they realised
he was gone.

"Conall!" they shouted. "Conall, speak to us!" And
when there was no reply they groped their way back and
tried to look around—although, for obvious reasons,
they were nervous of investigating too thoroughly without
a light.

"There is a shepherd's cottage over there," said
Peter, pointing in the direction of a tiny yellow beam.
"We could go and ask for help."

"I'm with you," agreed Benedict.

So they ran as fast as they could in the dark and
roused the shepherd, who gave them burning turf on
long sticks and came himself to help them look. For as
long as the turf light lasted they searched frantically, but
no sign of a hole could they see on the sheep-cropped
surface of the hill. At last, however, just before the
flickering light died, they came upon a flat stone that
looked as if it had very recently been relaid and brushed
over with clay.

"This must be where Conall vanished," whispered

Peter in a frightened voice.

"It's the Good Folk have taken him, I'd say," said the shepherd, shaking his head. "This is well known as a fairy hill."

Benedict and Peter shivered, but they knew they could do no more, and went sadly home to bed.

Of course, no-one can disappear without causing talk among their neighbours, and news of what had happened on the hill soon spread through the district. Some people scoffed and said that if Conall O'Grady had disappeared it was to America; others supposed that he had met with an accident of the ordinary sort, although it was hard to explain why no trace of his body was ever found. But those who believed that he had been taken away by the Good Folk soon had evidence of a kind to support their claim.

The following spring, a ring of bright blue grass sprang up around the flat stone on the hillside, contrasting vividly with the pale green turf all around. In summer blue flowers bloomed among the grass, and continued to do so for thirty years until Conall, if he had lived on earth, would have been seventy years old. Did he then re-enter the world of the living, or did his spirit, under the hill, fade away when he reached three score and ten? No-one could tell, but after that the blue flowers faded, and the grass grew green again around the stone on Ardagh Hill.

On Dean Swift's Tomb in St Patrick's Cathedral, Dublin

Here lies the body
Of Jonathan Swift,
Dean of this Cathedral,
where savage indignation
can lacerate his heart no more.
Go, traveller,
and if you can, imitate
his gallant fight for human liberty.

Mr Barry

Long ago, when the British ruled in Ireland, the largest Irish towns had barracks to house the British army. If a town was too small to have a barracks, its residents were obliged to provide food and shelter for the soldiers. A man of some importance was appointed billet master, and if a company of soldiers arrived in the town it was his job to make sure they had supper and beds for the night. Of course these military guests were unwelcome in Irish homes, not only because they were British. They were often dirty, lousy, smelly and rude as well.

Towards the end of the eighteenth century the billet master in the town of Fermoy was Mr Consadine, a stout, self-important lawyer with a fondness for whiskey and a pride in his sense of humour. He was assisted in his duties by his son, Tom. Mr Consadine was not best pleased one October evening, just as he was topping up his tumbler for the eighth time, to hear a messenger banging on his front door and shouting that a company of grenadiers was entering the town. Scarcely had the billet master put on his wig, taken a candle and hurried across the hall to his office than the soldiers were outside, feet stamping, swords clinking, voices already raised in complaint.

"Never welcome," muttered Mr Consadine as he scrabbled in a drawer for a bundle of official forms, "and least of all at this hour of the night. But there's no help for it, Tom. Open the door and let them in."

It took a long time to allocate lodgings and write out the billets—signed papers that the soldiers had to show to their grudging, sulky hosts. The officers were sent to the inn while the sergeants and corporals, who had a reputation for truculence, were dispatched to the houses of those who were not best friends with Mr Consadine. The ordinary soldiers were quartered with the poorer families, and at last only one remained, an apple-cheeked young man who had fallen asleep in the shadows, leaning against the wall. Alerted by the sudden silence, he shook himself awake and slouched over to the table where Mr Consadine, who had failed to notice him, was rolling up his list of names and addresses. They peered at each other in the candlelight.

"Begging your pardon, sir," said the soldier, pleasantly enough. "I hope you have a good billet for me?"

Mr Consadine was tired, and in the mood to see impudence where none was intended. His nose twitched and his eyes blinked rapidly behind his spectacles.

"Oh, you want a *good* billet, do you?" he replied sarcastically. "Surely we can provide a *good* billet for a gentleman like yourself." He pretended to consult his list, then went on, "Now, let me see. Would the biggest house in the district be good enough for you, I wonder? Tom! Make out a billet for this gentleman on Mr Barry of Cairn Thierna!"

If he hadn't still been half asleep, the soldier might have noticed the astonishment in Tom's rather vacant blue eyes. "On Mr Barry of Cairn Thierna, Father?"

"On Mr Barry of Cairn Thierna," repeated Mr Consadine, giving Tom a sly wink that the soldier didn't notice either. "Hasn't he the largest, finest house in this part of the country? On second thoughts, I'll make out the billet myself. What's your name, my man?"

"Nathan Smith, sir," replied the young man, and Mr Consadine wrote it down.

The grenadier put his billet in his pocket, shouldered his musket and knapsack, and left, with many words of gratitude. Mr Consadine and Tom could scarcely wait until he was out of the building before bursting into loud guffaws.

"Mr Barry of Cairn Thierna!" howled Tom. "That's a good one, Father!"

"Aye, a good billet indeed," chortled Mr Consadine. "The fine fellow will find every comfort at Mr Barry's place. Will you join me in a tumbler, Tom, before we get off to bed?"

And away went father and son, well pleased with themselves.

Meanwhile Nathan Smith, informed by Tom that Mr Barry's house was some way out of town on the Cork road, was trudging along by moonlight, looking hopefully for the lights of a large dwelling. All he could see, however, was the silhouette of a towering mountain ahead of him, and a few poor cabins by the roadside. Eventually he met a man, and asked him the way to Mr Barry's.

"To Mr Barry's?" repeated the man. "What Mr Barry would that be, now?"

"I can't say for sure," admitted Nathan, "because I can't read. But Mr What's-his-name the billet master wrote on my billet that I'm to lodge in a large house belonging to Mr Barry of—Cairn something, could it be?"

"What?" The man peered at the soldier in the darkness. "It wouldn't be Mr Barry of Cairn Thierna you're talking about, would it?"

"That's the one," agreed Nathan, relieved. But then, glimpsing an odd expression on the man's face, he added anxiously, "You do know where his house is, don't you?"

"In a manner of speaking." The man smiled, and Nathan wondered if he was about to say something else. But good will towards English soldiers was lacking in these parts, and the Irishman merely shrugged his shoulders. "Do you see that mountain ahead of you?" he asked. "That's Cairn Thierna. When you come to a great heap of stones at the top, you will be close to Mr Barry's house."

Nathan thanked the man and wished him good-night. But his heart sank and his steps were slow and weary as he trudged on towards the mountain. Just as he reached its foot, however, he heard the sharp clip-clop of a horse's hooves on the frosty road behind him, and turned to see a dark rider approaching under the moon. Soon a tall, cloaked gentleman on a grey horse drew level with him, and when poor Nathan again asked directions to Mr Barry's, replied, "I am Mr Barry. What can I do for you, friend?"

"I've got a billet on your house from the billet master at Fermoy," Nathan explained.

"Have you so?" said Mr Barry, showing neither annoyance nor surprise. "Then you'd better come with me. Catch hold of my horse's tail and we'll soon be at the top of the mountain."

Never had Nathan felt such relief. Eagerly he caught hold of the grey mare's tail, and was amazed how quickly he advanced up the mountainside. In no time at all, not even out of breath, he was standing outside a house finer than Mr Consadine's or any other in Fermoy. It was three storeys high, with battlements on top, and every window lighted as if to welcome an honoured guest.

Nathan was only a common foot-soldier, and he expected now to be directed to the kitchen. Instead, after Mr Barry had handed the horse's reins to a servant, he smiled at Nathan and said, "Come with me." The astonished soldier was escorted through the hall to a cosy parlour where a fire burned brightly on the hearth.

"May I see your billet?" asked Mr Barry, and laughed when he saw what was written on the paper Nathan gave him.

"I know this man Consadine," he said with a gleam in his dark eyes. "He likes a joke, and, as he will discover, so do I. I seem to remember that he keeps a fine herd of cows in a field at Carrickabrick. A good sirloin of beef makes an excellent supper, do you not think, Mr Smith?"

Nathan agreed that it did, whereupon Mr Barry rang a bell and had a whispered conversation with the servant who answered it.

The young soldier could scarcely believe his good luck. Within half an hour the table was laid, wine uncorked, and a smoking sirloin of roast beef was carried in. Encouraged by Mr Barry, Nathan made an excellent supper, having to loosen his belt when he was only half way through.

"I'm sure, sir, not even Mr Consadine's cows could produce such beef," he remarked, when at last he could eat no more. Mr Barry smiled broadly, and helped his guest to more wine.

Then there was talk, and whiskey punch, and more talk, and so pleasant was Mr Barry's company that Nathan scarcely noticed time passing. He was quite sorry when at length his host yawned, and rose to his feet.

"Sad as I am to part with you, Mr Smith," said Mr Barry, "I have to be away from here before daybreak, and you too have a journey to make. But before I show you to your room, do you see that bundle by the door? It is the hide of the cow I had killed for your supper, and I'll be obliged if tomorrow you will take it to Mr Consadine and tell him it is a gift from Barry of Cairn Thierna. Will you do that for me?"

"With pleasure, sir," said Nathan fervently as he picked up the hairy bundle, and, with thanks on his part and good wishes on Mr Barry's, they parted. Full of beef and good liquor, the soldier was soon asleep in a warm, comfortable bed.

That was not where he woke up, however. It was the sun that woke him, and for a sleepy moment Nathan thought it was shining through his bedroom window. But then something hairy touched his neck, and he realised that he was lying on his back in the heather, with a rolled-up cowhide for a pillow. His musket and knapsack lay beside him, and high above a lark was singing in the clear sky. Rubbing his eyes, Nathan sat up, then got to his feet and gazed around. Not only the panelled room and the feather bed he had fallen asleep in were gone: Mr Barry's fine house had also disappeared, and he was alone on the mountaintop beside a huge pile of stones. Far below Nathan could see the town of Fermoy on the bank of the river Blackwater, and borne on the wind he faintly heard a bugle call. Had it not been for the evidence of the cowhide, he would have concluded that his whole experience had been a dream.

There was no reason to linger. Throwing the cowhide over his shoulder, Nathan grabbed his belongings and began to scramble down the mountainside. It was much more difficult than it had been coming up with Mr Barry, but at last he was back on the Cork road again. As soon as he reached Fermoy he went to Mr Consadine's house and asked to see him. He was shown into the billet master's office.

Mr Consadine couldn't help grinning when he saw the soldier coming through the door with his hair dishevelled and bits of heather sticking to his red coat.

"Well, my fine fellow," he tittered, "what sort of entertainment did Mr Barry of Cairn Thierna provide for you? You had a comfortable night, I hope?"

"A most excellent night, sir," Nathan assured him truthfully. "Mr Barry is a most considerate, kind gentleman, and I'm grateful to you, too. There are not many billets like that one, to be sure."

"Oh, very amusing!" snapped Mr Consadine, who only enjoyed jokes if he was making them himself. "Now what's your business, and what in the world is that hairy thing you're carrying?"

Carefully Nathan laid Mr Consadine's gift from Mr Barry across a chair. "It's the hide of the cow that provided our supper, sir," he replied solemnly. "Mr Barry asked me to bring it, and to tell you that it is a gift from him."

The billet master stared. The last trace of his sneering grin had faded, and an uneasy expression appeared in his small eyes. "You are—um, jesting, I suppose?" he said uncertainly. But before Nathan could answer there was a commotion outside, the door flew open, and a small, dirty boy tumbled excitedly into the room.

"What do you want, Patrick?" demanded Mr Consadine irritably. "I pay you to mind my cows, not—"

But the boy interrupted, his eyes like saucers in his

grubby face.

"Oh, sir!" he cried. "You've been robbed! The best cow in the field is gone, and no-one's seen a hair of her since yesterday. But wait!" He caught sight of the cowhide, and advanced incredulously towards it. As if afraid that it would bite him, he touched it, then leaped back as if he had indeed been bitten.

"Sir!" he squealed. "That's her hide, wherever she is!"

"What?" exclaimed Mr Consadine, jumping to his feet. His podgy face was ashen. "Are you sure?"

"Aye, sir. Look!" Patrick pointed eagerly. "There are the two white spots on her back, and there's the place where she rubbed the hair off her shoulder last Martinmas—"

But Mr Consadine didn't need any more proof. His face had turned from the colour of ash to the colour of sage. His mouth was opening and shutting like a fish, his wig was awry, and he groped feebly for his chair.

"Has Mr Barry robbed you, sir?" asked Nathan in disbelief.

Mr Consadine seemed to be struggling for breath.

"He has robbed me, if that is possible," he said thickly. "As for you, soldier, you should tremble to think where you spent last night. Barry of Cairn Thierna has been dead for a hundred years, and his house is a pile of stones on top of the mountain."

The Blarney Stone

Four miles north of Cork stands Blarney Castle, where you can see one of the most famous stones, not only in Ireland, but in the whole world. Cormac MacCarthy had the castle built in the fifteenth century, and had certainly intended it to last, since its walls are over twenty-six metres high and three-and-a-half metres thick at the base—as thick as two tall men lying end to end! The castle is built entirely of solid stone.

The Blarney Stone itself is set high up on the castle wall, and is supposed to give the power of eloquence to everyone who kisses it. The legend may have begun with a tart remark made by Queen Elizabeth I of England when she was exhausted by the ceaseless chatter of Dermot MacCarthy, the castle's sixteenth-century owner, and peeved because he refused to hand the castle over to her.

To kiss the Blarney Stone you need a good head for heights. You must lean backwards over the battlements, holding onto a rail, and touch the smooth black stone with your lips. The nineteenth-century poet Francis Mahony, also known as "Father Prout", was born at Cork, and wrote this verse about the Blarney Stone:

> There is a stone there
> That whoever kisses,

113

Oh, he never misses
To grow eloquent.
'Tis he may clamber
To a lady's chamber,
or become a member
Of Parliament.

The Murderer and the Angry Bones

ೲ

It was spring on Lewis, with cloud and sunlight and a fresh, gleeful wind. Up on the moors the grouse were hatching their young, and it seemed only sensible to Abe and Willie to take a day off school and go egg-collecting. In another week or two it would be too late. Sneaking out of Stornoway one morning they made for the moors, and had a pleasant time searching for nests among the heather. But when it was time to go home, and they discovered that Willie had taken twice as many eggs as Abe, a bitter quarrel broke out.

"It isn't fair. We took the same risk playing truant, so we should each get half," said Abe sullenly.

"Why should we," retorted Willie, "when I'm twice as clever as you?"

There was just enough truth in this to raise Abe's hackles. "You are not clever," he growled, glaring at Willie's hands, which were full of eggs. "You're just greedy and mean."

Willie scowled. "Say it again and I'll punch you in the face."

"Right, then. I'll fight you for the lot."

So the eggs were laid aside, and a moment later the two boys were fighting furiously, first on their feet and then down on the heather. They pummelled each other, and scratched and kicked until they were nearly exhausted.

The quarrel would probably have ended then, and the eggs been shared after all, if Willie hadn't unwisely called Abe stupid again. Abe wasn't a wicked boy but he had a ferocious temper. Too enraged to foresee the consequences, he staggered to his feet, picked up a sharp stone, and brought it crashing down on his companion's skull. Willie died instantaneously.

Abe was horrified by what he had done, but when he thought that he would surely be hanged, he determined to hide his crime if he could. Close by there was a large white stone, excavated on its seaward side by the tireless wind, so that at its base there was a hollow like a little cave. Beating down feelings of terror and revulsion, Abe dragged Willie's body to the stone, packed it into the hollow, and covered it thickly with earth and gravel. Then he vanished among the heather.

Hiding by day and walking warily by night, the unhappy youth made his way south to Tarbert in Harris. There he persuaded a fisherman to take him to the mainland, and travelled to Glasgow. By the time the search for the missing boys had been sadly abandoned on Lewis, the murderer was sailing out of the Clyde estuary on a merchant ship bound for America.

It is a terrible thing to be afraid to go home. For twenty-five years Abe roamed the world, visiting faraway, exotic lands but yearning always for his father and mother and the windswept island where he had been born. He was a skilful sailor but an unpopular man, always dour and solitary. Still, no-one could have guessed the dreadful secret that made him so. Wherever he went Abe had an unseen companion, the schoolboy he had murdered in the heather long ago. Willie's reproachful eyes encountered his in dark places, and he was sick at heart with guilt and remorse.

Then one day, he did go back to Lewis. The ship he was sailing in needed a repair, and its captain decided to put in at Stornoway. Abe had no choice in the matter.

As the sun went down, Abe stood at the ship's rail, watching the lights come on in the little town. Now that he was here, Stornoway was the last place on earth he wanted to be, yet he was filled with curiosity. A quarter of a century had passed, and he thought it improbable that anyone would recognise the black-bearded, sunburnt sailor as the pink-faced schoolboy who had disappeared on that fateful spring day so long ago. Surely it would be safe to take a walk through the narrow streets and stand once more outside the house where he had lived? It was unlikely that he would ever have the chance again.

As if in a dream he had had a thousand times, Abe walked down the gangway and passed into the town. At first little seemed to have changed. There was the school, there was the kirk, and there was the shop where his mother used to buy bread. But when Abe arrived at the street where he had been brought up, a surprise awaited him, and he didn't know whether to be glad or sorry. His parents' house had been demolished, and on the site stood an inn. The fragrance of cooking fish reminded him that he was hungry, and he went in and ordered a meal.

The landlady was a friendly woman who responded willingly to Abe's careful questions. Yes, she said, there had been a house there until a few years ago, but it had fallen into disrepair after the deaths of the people who owned it. The landlady was a newcomer to the island, but she believed there had been some tragedy in their lives. A child—or was it children?—had disappeared, oh, many years ago. No-one had wanted to live in the house after them for fear of bad luck, so at last it had been pulled down.

When the woman went off to fetch his supper, Abe sat staring at the checked tablecloth, numb with grief. Not only was he a murderer but he had broken his parents' hearts as well. *I wish I were dead too,* he thought.

Abe's mind was far away as he idly picked up the knife and fork the landlady had placed before him, but as he fingered them a strangeness in their shape made him frown and examine the white handles more closely. As he was doing so the landlady reappeared with a steaming dish of herring and potatoes. Her husband followed with a tankard of ale.

"Well," beamed the landlady as she put down the dish. "I'm pleased to see you admiring the handles of my cutlery. I made them myself, as a matter of fact."

"Did you?" replied Abe, making an effort to be polite.

"Yes, indeed," said the landlady, and she began to tell a tale that slowly froze Abe's heart. "I was coming home late one evening from Balallan, and sat down by the big white stone beyond Soval to take a piece of grit out of my shoe. Something whitish under the stone attracted my attention, so I went to have a look. The wind and rain had worn away the earth, and there were four white bones sticking up—from a dead sheep, I dare say. So I brought them home and made new handles for some old knives and—"

The woman broke off abruptly, alarmed by the expression of horror on her guest's face. But it was her husband, who had gone very pale, who pointed with a shaking finger and whispered, "Good God, man! What's the matter with your hands? They're all smeared with blood!"

As these fatal words were uttered, Abe felt the bone handles move in his grasp, and with a howl he let them fall onto the table. There was blood on the cloth too.

"These are not sheep's bones," he cried. "They're poor Willie's bones, and I murdered him. His angry bones bear witness against me!"

The landlord's hand closed firmly on Abe's shoulder.

It was a great relief to Abe to confess to the crime that had blackened his life for twenty-five years. He had no wish to live longer, and met his death bravely on Gallows Hill.

Ever since, the white stone between Stornoway and Loch Seaforth has been haunted at the eerie hours by the ghost of a boy. But which boy? No-one seeing the apparition has ever stayed long enough to find out.

A Stony Island

❀

Far out in the Atlantic Ocean, fifty-five miles west of the Outer Hebrides, are the lonely islands of St Kilda, among the stoniest on earth. No trees grow in such windswept places, and the islanders who lived there from Neolithic times until 1930, when the last of them left for the mainland, were dependent for all their building needs on stone.

They built their houses of stone, and used boulders on the ends of ropes to hold down the thatch. They built stone storehouses, and larders called cleits. The remains of three stone churches can be seen, as well as standing stones associated with a religion older than Christianity. The St Kildans were very religious, but, like all people who live close to the elements, very superstitious too. Not surprisingly, many of their superstitions had stone connections. Here are two, recorded by Rev. Kenneth MacAuley, whose history of St Kilda was published in 1764.

On the main island of St Kilda stood a large, square, white stone with a hollowed top. The supernatural being who guarded the stone was called the gruagach. Once she had been a woman of good family, but having been put under a spell she became a kind of fairy—a relation, perhaps, of the glaistigs of the mainland. The gruagach too was interested in cattle and the dairy, and on Sundays the islanders took offerings of milk to her stone and poured them into the hollow on top. They hoped that this would encourage the gruagach to protect their cattle from disease and ensure a good supply of milk, butter, and cheese.

Another stone that the islanders cherished was called the clach dotaig. This was a small, semi-transparent stone believed to protect its owner against misfortune, illness, and accident. To obtain this "stone of virtues" was very difficult. First you had to steal a raven's egg from its nest, boil the egg hard, and return it to the nest when the raven wasn't looking. Then you had to hide, and wait for the raven to get tired of sitting on an egg that wouldn't hatch. When that happened, the raven would lose its temper, fly off, and return with a clach dotaig, intending to drop it and break the shell of the hard-boiled egg. At that point you had to jump out, frighten the raven, and snatch the stone as a lucky charm.

The Soup Stone

෧෩

Not so very long ago there lived a poor man whose name was Séamas O'Hare. Summer and winter he travelled the roads of Ireland, and while in summer he loved to be out of doors, tramping in sunshine and sleeping under the stars, in winter he was often cold and hungry.

One bitter January day, when icicles hung everywhere and the sun had no warmth to melt them, Séamas blew on his raw hands and thought that a bowl of soup was what he'd like more than anything in the world. There was a farm nearby, but the farmer's wife was a hard woman, who had chased Séamas out of the yard once before. Still, he thought, with a little luck and cleverness this time he could get what he wanted.

So down went Séamas to the side of the river, and there among the frosty stones he found one that was round, smooth, and the size of a small apple. Putting it in his pocket, he strode up the road to the farmhouse and knocked at the door.

"Good morning, ma'am," he said politely to the farmer's wife when she opened the door a crack. "I was wondering if you could let me have a drop of hot water and the loan of a scrubbing brush?"

"Oh, and what would you be wanting that for?" demanded the woman suspiciously, peering sharply at Séamas's ragged clothes and broken boots. She didn't remember his face, since she never bothered to look at beggars she chased away from her door.

"Just for a small job I have to do," replied Séamas, civil and mysterious at the same time.

If he had asked her for food, the woman would have shut the door. But because it would cost her nothing, she handed out some hot water in a saucepan and a small brush. Séamas thanked her, sat down on the doorstep, and fell to washing and scrubbing and polishing his stone until it shone like a jewel. He knew the farmer's wife was watching him from the kitchen window, but he paid no attention. He was not surprised, however, when after a while she opened the door again.

"You're having a lot of work cleaning that stone, my man," she observed, poking her long nose into the frosty air. This was the moment he was waiting for.

"Yes, indeed, ma'am," he replied seriously. "You see, it's a soup stone."

"A soup stone?" The woman repeated the words with a puzzled frown. "Are you saying you can make soup with it?"

Séamas smiled. "The best soup in the world," he said.

The farmer's wife was silent a moment, and Séamas went on polishing the stone on his tattered cuff. Then she said, "And—could anyone do it?"

"Anyone," Séamas assured her. "All they have to do is first watch the one who knows how it's done." He paused for a moment, then added innocently: "Would you be wanting a lesson, ma'am?"

The woman's eyes gleamed greedily. "I'd be greatly obliged to you," she said, opening the door wide and beckoning Séamas into the kitchen. "There's the pot and there's the fire, and plenty of water in the jug behind the door."

She sat down in her chair and watched Séamas intently as he put water in the pot, dropped the stone into it, and put another turf on the fire. Then he too sat down and warmed himself. The two of them watched the pot, and after a while it came to the boil.

"A shake of salt and pepper would do no harm," remarked Séamas when he had tasted the water with a spoon. So the woman gave him the salt and pepper, and Séamas seasoned the pot. Time ticked by, and after another while he tasted the water again.

"Hmm. It isn't thickening as well as it should," he admitted, licking his lips. "A shake of flour would do it no harm." The farmer's wife nodded, and fetched a good handful of flour from the crock. She sprinkled it over the pot herself, and gave it a stir.

"Oh, and that mutton bone you've laid aside for the dog's dinner has plenty of meat on it," said Séamas, as if he'd just thought if it. "It would do the soup no harm, but improve it maybe." The woman didn't like to say that she had really laid it aside for her husband's supper, so into the pot it went.

"There'll be great strength in the soup now," Séamas said with satisfaction, "though to tell the truth, a few potatoes would do no harm." So what did the silly woman do but fetch a knife, peel six large potatoes, and cut them up for the pot!

"It's thickening nicely now," Séamas told her, tasting it again with the spoon and sniffing the rich, soupy smell. "But do you not think yourself that a couple of these nice big onions you have on the table would finish it nicely?"

No sooner said than done. Amazed at being able to make soup from a stone, the farmer's wife eagerly peeled and chopped the onions, and threw them into the pot. Then she sat down, and Séamas sat down, and for half an hour the soup simmered away, getting stronger and thicker and more tasty.

At last Séamas got up, stirred the pot, and decided that the soup would do. "It's ready now," he told the woman. "Maybe you'd like a taste of it?"

"Oh, just a tiny drop," she cried delightedly, hurrying to get down two large bowls from the shelf and ladling a huge helping into each of them. "This is fine soup," she added, as Séamas drew his chair to the table. "I'm much obliged to you for showing me how to make it."

"Ah, didn't I tell you," grinned Séamas, "that you could make the finest soup in all the world from a good soup stone?"

And after he had had a second helping and a pipe of her husband's tobacco, he said goodbye to the farmer's wife and went on his way.

Of course the farmer's wife couldn't help boasting about how she could make soup out of a stone, and her neighbours couldn't help laughing at her foolishness. Séamas laughed too, but decided that it would be wise to travel elsewhere in the country for some time to come.

Tintock-Tap

❧

On Tintock-tap there is a mist,
And in that mist there is a kist,
And in the kist there is a caup,
And in the caup there is a drap;
Tak up the caup, drink aff the drap,
And set the caup on Tintock-tap.

Kate Niven's Hoard

◎◎

Between Dillerhill and Crossfoord,
There lies Katie Neevie's hoord.

Everyone in the parish of Lesmahagow in Lanarkshire knew the rhyme, and everyone believed it to be true. In the middle of a field on Clerkston farm there stood an immense black stone, marking the burial-place of "a bootful, a kettleful and a bullhideful of gold". The gold had been the property of Mrs Kate Niven or "Katie Neevie", as she had been familiarly known, who had lived at Clerkston centuries ago; no-one was sure exactly when. Why she had chosen to put her money in such a place was mysterious, and there was little chance of finding out, but anyway to the good folk of Lesmahagow it was of little importance. What mattered was that gold, by the bootful, kettleful, and bullhideful, was there for the taking, if only—

But there was a snag. Of course, over the centuries resourceful people had tried to get their hands on what was now of small use to Mrs Niven. Dreaming of gold, lusting after it and planning how to spend it were universal pastimes in the parish. Unfortunately all attempts to find it had been in vain, for the terrible reason that the treasure had a guardian—none other than Old Hornie, the enemy of mankind, the Devil himself.

127

Appalling tales had been passed down the generations of how, just as the treasure-seekers struck at the base of the stone with their spades, this well-known being had jumped out on them, lashing his scaly tail and breathing intolerable flame into their faces. His eyes like coals of fire, his razor-sharp fangs, and his evil leer had been described so often that by the middle of the nineteenth century no-one dared go near the stone at all. Dreaming of the bootful, the kettleful, and the bullhideful went on, but attempts to get at the treasure had long since been abandoned.

Then a new tenant arrived at Clerkston. He was Mr Prentice, a cynical, cunning farmer who believed neither in the Devil nor in Kate Niven's hoard. What annoyed him was the presence of an enormous stone in the middle of his best field. It got in the way of the plough and occupied land that Mr Prentice, a tight-fisted fellow, could have put to better use.

"Old Hornie will get you if you disturb the stone," warned his neighbours, half-fearful and half-hopeful, since Mr Prentice was not making himself well liked in the parish.

"Superstitious old women, the lot of you," was the farmer's scornful reply.

All through his first year at Clerkston, Mr Prentice scowled on Kate Niven's stone, but it wasn't until late summer that he thought of a plan for getting rid of it. At that time it was usual for itinerant Irishmen to come over to Scotland looking for work at harvest time. Like most other farmers, Mr Prentice was pleased to have their labour, and paid them next to nothing for it. This year there were five Irishmen at Clerkston, and on the night of the kirn-supper, or harvest-home, he called them into the kitchen.

"You have all worked well," said he, "and it occurs to me that I might do you a favour. You know that black stone in the middle of my great field?" The men nodded solemnly.

"Under it," Mr Prentice went on, "there lie a bootful, a kettleful, and a bullhideful of gold, buried in Queen Mary's time, I think it was." The labourers' eyes widened greedily, but Mr Prentice shook his head.

"I don't know that I should suggest you go looking for it, though," he said. "The breaking of the stone would tax your strength, and—well, never mind. Forget I mentioned it."

The poor men fell straight into his trap. "And what?" they cried. "Why should we not be looking for it, sir? Tell us, now."

So, pretending reluctance, Mr Prentice told them about Old Hornie, with his scaly tail and fiery eyes and his breath that could take the skin off your face. He could see the conflict in their eyes, between the desire for gold, which could make their miserable lives worth living, and fear of the Devil, who had foiled all previous attempts to take it. He thought he knew how to tip the balance.

"No-one would blame you for not taking such a risk," he said, shrugging his shoulders, "when you can make a good living by hard work."

That did it. The Irishmen thought of the living they could make by hard work, and made up their minds.

"I'll do it!" said one.

"I'm with you!" said another.

"Yes!"

"Yes!"

"And I'll borrow a gun," said the last man stoutly.

"We'll take turns to stand guard, boys, and see how the Devil runs with a burst of shot in his behind!"

So next morning the five Irishmen went out to the field with picks, hammers, and a shotgun for protection, and by noon they had hacked the black stone to pieces. Delighted to have the stone removed from his land without paying for the work, Mr Prentice stood laughing in the yard. Then, whistling to his dog, he went into the house and locked the door.

Certainly the Irishmen received no visit from the Devil, for which no doubt they were properly thankful. Whether they found Kate Niven's hoard is an open question, for they were never seen in the district again after that day. But it was reported that a man coming home from Lanark met them on the road, carrying a sack and with broad smiles on their faces.

Fyvie, Findhaven, and Thomas the Rhymer

❧

Thomas of Ercildoun, also known as "True Thomas" and "Thomas the Rhymer", lived in the thirteenth century in Scotland, where he is even better known as a prophet than the Brahan Seer. An old ballad tells how Thomas was carried off by the Fairy Queen; he lived for seven years in her kingdom, and was believed to have acquired there the magic powers that made him famous. Although usually associated with the Border land where he was born, Thomas travelled widely. Two of his prophecies concern castles of the north.

Thomas arrived at Fyvie Castle in Aberdeenshire in the middle of a storm of rain and wind so ferocious that it stripped the leaves from the surrounding forest and slammed the castle gates against him. Soaked to the skin and with a venom worthy of the Brahan Seer, he cursed the castle with these words:

> *Fyvie, Fyvie, thou shalt never thrive,*
> *As lang as there's in thee stanes three:*
> *There's ane within the highest tower,*
> *There's ane within the ladye's bower,*
> *There's ane within the water-yett,*
> *And thir three stanes ye sall never get.*

Tradition says that two of the stones were found, but the third, beneath the gate or "yett" leading to the river Ythan, has so far eluded discovery. Fyvie has thrived well enough, however; today it is one of the stateliest castles in the north, and is owned by the National Trust for Scotland.

Time has been less kind to Findhaven Castle in Angus, of which Thomas the Rhymer said,

> *When Findhaven Castle rins to sand,*
> *The warld's end is near at hand.*

A strong, busy fortress in medieval times, Findhaven is now a sad, lonely ruin. Two-thirds of its south wall have crumbled, and although the north wall still stands, slowly but surely its stones are disintegrating. Certainly they will one day "rin to sand", and test the truth of Thomas's prophecy.

The Lost Sheep

Many years ago, near Mitchelstown in County Cork, there lived a poor man called Gorman. One day when he was working in his potato patch two things happened simultaneously; his spade struck stone and, more astonishingly, he heard a sheep bleating somewhere below his feet. Hastily shovelling away some earth, Gorman uncovered a flat expanse of stone with a wide hole in the middle. He realised that a sheep had fallen through. Reckoning that the value of fleece and flesh was worth the risk, he lowered himself through the hole, and found a frightened ewe stranded on a rocky ledge just below the surface.

Gorman was a strong man, and with little effort he heaved the sheep up into the sunlight. She went on bleating piteously, and when he saw that she had broken a leg in her fall, Gorman took her up across his shoulders and carried her to his cabin nearby. It was his intention to make mutton of her immediately, but the creature looked up at him so appealingly that he couldn't bring himself to kill her. His wife, who was a kind woman, straightened the broken leg and bound it up. The sheep was fed and, in the course of time, was able to walk again.

As if to show her gratitude for the Gormans' kindness, the following spring the rescued ewe produced two strong lambs, from whom a fine flock grew. Their wool was like silk, so precious that it fetched at market four times as much as ordinary wool, and the Gormans prospered beyond their wildest dreams. The old cabin was replaced with a grand house, old clothes with new ones, tea and potatoes with wine and meat.

Sadly, however, as Gorman grew richer he also grew greedier and less kind. As time passed, the original sheep, now the great-grandmother of the flock, became old and feeble, and one day the ungrateful man decided to kill her, and eat her on St Martin's Day. His wife was horrified and did her best to dissuade him, but the nasty Gorman told her loudly to be quiet.

"The sheep is useless and not worth her keep," he said hard-heartedly. "I'll kill her myself tomorrow morning."

And no doubt he would have kept his word, if the sheep hadn't had other ideas. When Gorman rose next morning and went to the field to fetch his victim, a surprise awaited him. Every single sheep had run away! Of course Gorman was furious, and frightened too, for the flock was his wealth.

All day long he scoured the countryside, and his relief may be imagined when, as evening drew on, he found the sheep huddled in the lee of a hill, with the poor old great-grandmother standing in the middle. None too kindly, Gorman drove them home, but they came quietly with never a hint of malice in their mild eyes.

But to get home they had to go through Gorman's old potato patch, and as they passed the hole in the stone from which, in gentler days, he had rescued the injured ewe, one by one the sheep slipped down into it. It happened so quickly, that Gorman might as well have thought of catching last year's snow as of gripping even one of the silky fleeces. He stood aghast as his fine livelihood vanished from his sight.

Then, shouting wildly for his neighbours to bring lights, Gorman went down the hole after the sheep. Beyond the ledge it was pitch dark, and the stupid man blundered about, roaring for the creatures to come and be killed. But the only response was the mocking echo of his own voice.

When Gorman's neighbours arrived with rushlights, they found to their amazement the most wonderful caves, vaulted and pillared like the palace of a goblin king. The caves can still be seen near Mitchelstown today, but Gorman's sheep were gone for ever.

The Fire of Stones

Witches in the north of Ireland knew how to make a curse that would last. On the cold hearth a pile of pebbles was built, and an eggshell filled with water was carefully placed on top. Then the curser would concentrate on the victim and say, "May you never have luck until this fire of stones boils the water in this eggshell."

Fergus O'Mara and the Air-Demons

∾∾

Of all the wicked goblins that pestered the people of Ireland long ago, none were feared and hated as much as the air-demons. These loathsome beings lived in high rocks among the clouds and mist, and took every opportunity to harm innocent humans in their vicinity. Sometimes they drove people mad with fear.

On the southern slope of the Ballyhoura Mountains in County Cork lived a farmer, Fergus O'Mara, whose misfortune it was to live close by a little hill, covered with trees apart from the rocky summit, which protruded like a bald head from the leaves. On stormy nights dreadful noises could be heard coming from the rock: screaming and screeching and loud, devilish laughter. Everyone knew that the rock was a haunt of air-demons and avoided it, not least Fergus, who had once been told by a holy monk that the air-demons had a strong desire to destroy him.

"As long as you lead a good life and go to Mass on Sundays you will be safe," the monk had said. "But if ever you forget God, or fall into sin, you will be in great danger. Never forget that the air-demons are watching you night and day."

This was an uncomfortable thought, but fortunately Fergus was by nature a good man, who attended Mass every Sunday because he wanted to. But if ever he was tempted to do something bad, the monk's warning quickly persuaded him to change his mind.

Fergus had a loving wife and children, but there had been one great sadness in his life. A little daughter had died, and even the patient, godly manner of her death couldn't take away the pain of losing her. Fergus often thought about the little girl, and puzzled over her insistence, as she lay dying, that a blessed candle should be placed in her hands. It had seemed a strange request, but the child had pleaded earnestly and had of course been granted her wish. Holding the candle, she had died peacefully, with a smile on her lips.

About a year after his daughter's death, on a rain-washed spring morning, Fergus was about to set out for Mass. There was no church in the district at the time, and Mass was celebrated in the open air at an ancient fort, three miles from the O'Mara farm. Mrs O'Mara and the children had left home some time before. Fergus, who could walk faster, had stayed behind to finish some chores. Now he too was ready to leave.

The way to Lissanaffrin, the fort of the Mass, lay first through fields, then uphill through wood, skirting the air-demons' infamous rock. Fergus was enjoying the beauty of the morning, admiring the opening buds and listening to birdsong, when unexpectedly a huge stag bounded out of the trees in front of him. Three yelping hounds eagerly hurtled after. Fergus was a fanatical huntsman; above all else he loved the chase, and the sight of deer and hounds roused in him a passionate desire to follow. Forgetting that it was Sunday and that he was on his way to Mass, Fergus dashed after the hounds. Away and away he ran, uphill and downhill, over rocks, through thickets, and across streams, until he was hot and wet and his best clothes were covered with dirt and dead winter leaves.

Sometimes Fergus seemed to be in reach of the dogs' tails; at other times both deer and hounds leaped far ahead of him. But so keen on the chase was he that he allowed himself to be led over hills and through glens, forgetting his duty to God, forgetting the monk's solemn warning, and never pausing to wonder to whom these tireless animals belonged. At last, too exhausted to go on, he fell far behind, and saw both stag and hounds vanish across a desolate moor.

Sinking wearily onto a stone, Fergus was suddenly stricken by the realisation of his own folly and, as if to emphasise it, the baying of the departing hounds took on a new yet familiar tone. To his horror, Fergus recognised the shrieks of wicked laughter he had so often heard coming from the air-demons' rock, and knew that he had fallen into a trap. The cunning demons had lured him away from Mass, and now he was miles from home, endangered by the demons' malevolence and his own ungodly choice.

"I must get home before nightfall," Fergus told himself, and, spurred by fear, he began to walk as fast as he could in the direction of his farm.

For a while all seemed to be well. Fergus knew the mountain paths, and even as night fell and the wind rose he stepped forward on confident feet. At last he saw the light from his own kitchen shining in the dark, and trudged eagerly towards it, forgetting in his relief that he still had to pass the air-demons' rock. He was reminded by a sudden drop in the temperature and a new keening in the wind.

The storm struck in an instant. One minute Fergus

was on course, the next bewildered by the stinging rain. Thunder growled, and in a livid flash of lightning he saw a large black cloud detach itself from the top of the demons' rock. As it hurtled in his direction, Fergus crossed himself, but even as he tried to dash for home the cloud moved in front of him, blocking his path. Sobbing with terror, the poor man saw that the dark vapour was full of ghastly, leering faces, all staring at him with evil, bloodshot eyes. The cloud came spinning towards him, its vile substance ready to enfold him.

But then, just as Fergus gave himself up for lost, a light appeared in the sky. Descending like a swiftly falling star, it positioned itself in front of the demon-cloud.

Daring to lift his eyes, Fergus was amazed to see his little daughter floating in the air between him and the demons. The wind howled and the rain poured, but the child hovered serenely in the eye of the storm, smiling at her father in the light of the candle she held steadily in her small hands. Even in his anguish Fergus observed that all traces of sickness had vanished from her face, and as their eyes met he felt a quick, piercing joy. But the demons screamed with even greater fury. Fergus saw them draw back momentarily from the holy light, but then they whirled wildly round in their cloud to his unprotected side. Yet wherever they tried to attack him, the child with the candle was there, floating unperturbed in between.

Seeing the possibility of escape, Fergus found new strength and ran; the demons followed in a tempest that tore down branches and uprooted trees. More than once Fergus thought he was done for, but always the little girl placed herself between her father and the evil spirits, to guide him safely home.

Fortunately Mrs O'Mara was a woman of faith. Sure that her husband would return, she had left the door open, and was brave enough not to close it as the demon-storm approached. Suddenly Fergus shot through, leaped into the middle of the kitchen, and collapsed on the floor. Immediately, though no-one had touched it, the door was slammed and its heavy bolts driven home. Mrs O'Mara and the children rushed to lift Fergus up, deaf in their relief to the din of demons howling in frustration around the house, although their neighbours cowered trembling in their beds. Gradually, however, the uproar receded and finally died away. The clouds rolled back, the moon rose and peace settled back over the land.

Fergus lay unconscious of noise and quiet. It was next morning before he woke, and many days passed before he recovered from his dreadful experience. Only the knowledge that he had been rescued by his little child, and that she was happy, made it bearable at all.

The devastation around the house took even longer to mend. Trees and bushes were mangled, thatch was torn from the roof, and the garden lay in ruin. But the noise of air-demons was never heard again from the rock. In their disappointment they deserted it, and went to find a new haunt elsewhere.

From "Under Ben Bulben" by W B Yeats

∽

Under bare Ben Bulben's head
In Drumcliff churchyard Yeats is laid.
An ancestor was rector there
Long years ago, a church stands near,
By the road an ancient cross.
No marble, no conventional phrase;
On limestone quarried near the spot
By his command these words are cut:

Cast a cold eye
On life, on death.
Horseman, pass by!

Also by Poolbeg

Tales of St Columba

By

Eileen Dunlop

Nearly fifteen hundred years ago a man of royal blood was born in Gartan in the heart of Donegal in the north of Ireland. To the world outside he is known as St Columba but the Irish preferred to call him Colm Cille—the Dove of the Church. He was prince and saint, scholar and statesman, and for centuries after his death people told stories about his nobility, his courage, his pride and his miracles.

Why did this prince become a holy monk? Why did this monk leave the country he loved to exile himself on the windswept Scottish island of Iona? The life of the historical Columba is as marvellous as the stories of wonder told about him and Eileen Dunlop, one of Scotland's leading children's authors, is the ideal guide to both the legend and the man.

Tales of St Columba is an entrancing book.

Also by Poolbeg

Duck and Swan

By

John Quinn

When Martin "Duck" Oduki, abandoned in Dublin by a Nigerian father and Irish mother runs away from St Mark's Care Centre, Emer Healy discovers him hiding on a school bus bound for Galway.

Watching her sick mother's struggle to regain her health, Emer is also running from the pain and confusion she feels inside. It isn't long before the two children discover they need each other.

Duck finds other unusual allies in Granny Flynn, who knows a thing or two about institutional life, and her husband, blind Tom, who introduces Duck to the game of hurling.

Duck and Swan is a moving and often funny story of friendship and acceptance set against a background of intolerance and high adventure in a quiet part of County Galway.